MAGICK

The Unwanted Series, Book I

C. M. NEWELL

MAGICK, The Unwanted Series, Book I

(2nd Edition)

An eBook Me Up Publication by arrangement with the author.

Copyright © 2020 by C. M. Newell

Cover Designer Maria Spada

All rights reserved.

Hard Cover Print ISBN: 978-0-9976836-5-3

Print ISBN: 978-0-9976836-2-2

eBook ISBN: 978-0-9976836-1-5

CONTENT WARNINGS

Attempted Assault
Bullying Behavior
Death, Murder

To my rogue guardian, Butch.
My forever warrior and partner.

MAGICK

CONTENTS

REIGN

PART I

The girl calls to fate.
Fate is silent and watchful.

CHAPTER 1

My mother died when I was six years old. My father and others labeled it "the accident," but my life and his were never quite the same after. Today I'm looking into the eyes of my newest psychiatrist, retelling the same old story of the accident. Although in truth, that's not even the reason I'm stuck talking to a shrink. Not this time.

It's different talking to him instead of Dr. Bauche. She transferred me to him—something about a specialty and trying something new before the court-appointed therapy ended. His dark blue eyes are kind and thoughtful; he prefers I use his first name. Trying to be relatable to a teenager, I suppose.

"You've become disconnected in retelling your accident. Is this all your memory or what others have told you, Willow?" he asks.

"Well, it happened a long time ago. Part is from what my father and others told me, and part is what I pieced together." I gauge his reaction, which reveals nothing. Then he writes something on his notepad. I hate the writing in the notebook part; it feels judgmental.

"Have you ever undergone regressive therapy, to learn more about the accident?"

"No! Why would I want to do that?" I move further back into the chaise lounge and hug my arms tight. I guess we're going to be on the "accident" topic for the next sessions. Why do I always end up back there?

"That isn't why I have to come here," I stammer.

"I'm aware of the incident with the boy."

"You mean the potential rapist." I shiver at the thought of being pulled into that dark alley with his breath on the nape of my neck, he hands are grabbing and touching me, asking if I was scared, taunting me.

"Let's not call it rape, it was an assault. Willow, I don't fault you, but it is a mystery about how he got hurt. Did that boy simply get what was coming to him? That's not for me to decide. I'm here to address the anger issue the judge perceived you couldn't control during the trial."

The boy attacked me and pushed me to push back, and I did. Granted, I don't remember the outcome of his arm breaking and the fact he caught fire,—too damn bad his victim turned it on him, and he was injured. Serves him right! That boy's lawyer berated me, the victim, for their gain. We won the case, but it didn't feel like winning. My outburst when that boy said I wanted it and asked for it—set me off, it felt appropriate when I hit that lawyer. He got up in my face and wouldn't back down. The judge disagreed and although Daddy Dearest gave a payout in closed court proceedings, counseling for the trauma was part of the court appointed deal.

"It's been almost two years from the assault and I haven't had any issues. Anger is appropriate for a teenager," I snap.

Closing his notebook, Dr. Evan put it on the side table next to his chair. Leaning forward, he clasped his hands on his crossed leg.

"Addressing the accident where your mother died would help with your last year in high school, Willow. There are a lot of pressures. The accident is important for you to understand, in order to face your future."

A burst of air leaves my lungs in a short, sarcastic huff.

My response takes him by surprise. Apparently he hasn't met or talked to my father to know my future is mapped out. Did he read the previous notes from Dr. Bauche? A prestigious business school is awaiting me —most likely Harvard, my father being an alumnus and financial contributor. I can smell the old dusty hypocrisy waft in the air.

"Something funny?" Dr. Evan raises his eyebrow and smirks.

"I just . . . my future is an expectation." I grin without joy. "The legacy of a Warrington, you know?" It would be a tough one to live up too, with a grandfather and father who took the world financial market of acquisitions and mergers by storm.

I look around the office distractedly. Dr. Evan's bare, modern, steel-and-glass desk sits in the opposite corner, a red light blinking on the desk phone. The bookcase behind the desk is too far to focus on the books displayed. No pictures or diplomas hang on the light gray walls. The only fixture to pay attention to is Dr. Evan.

"Your father has agreed to my treatment plan and is aware of this approach," he says. "Talk with him, and let's plan on scheduling the session early next week."

Did I want to relive the accident? Ah, no thank you. Been there, done that. Before getting into that discussion, a timer signals that the session is over—saved by the bell.

Thank god.

"Goddess," he mumbles.

"Huh?"

"We'll talk about this more next session. Let's make our opportunities together count," he says as he walks me to the door of his office.

I wave goodbye to the familiar receptionist on the phone, who hits the buzzer that allows me out of the office. Security for entering, security for leaving. It is a prison, ironically.

I get into the elevator, push the button for the ground floor, and exhale. Leaving the building, I pass Dr. Bauche. She has a puzzled look on her face.

"Hello, Willow."

I respond with a polite smile.

Only a few more sessions with Dr. Evan and I'm done. Free!

I walk to my car in the empty parking garage, slip into the driver's seat, and lock the doors. My own space on my own terms. I open my Coach purse and reach for my phone; I have text messages from Daniel, my boyfriend, and Lucy, my best friend.

Lucy confirms that she is picking me up for school tomorrow, and Daniel is being typical, lovable Daniel with a simple text that says, *I love you can't wait to see you.*

I smile to myself and drive into the early evening, toward the Warrington mausoleum of home sweet home.

CHAPTER 2

K *nock knock.*

"I'm up. Getting dressed," I announce.

"Good. Your father wanted to make sure. Break-fast is ready when you are. Big day!" Mrs. Scott, the house manager, sounds too awake for normal, un-caffeinated people.

I sit up and stretch, wishing I could lie back down for a minute.

"Be there in a few," I reply.

I step into my walk-in closet and take my school uniform off the hanger. I'm happy this is the last year I'll have to wear that boring blue skirt. The skirt and the white button-down oxford with the prestigious Trinity Cross School logo proudly displayed on the left chest will be retired soon, along with Chepstow, Massachusetts in my rearview mirror. I slip my feet into my purple Chucks, breaking the blue-and-white uniform school rule. My personal rebellion. I open my door and Duke, my black lab, runs past me, his stomach leading the way for both of us. He paws down the back stairs of the house, turning left through the small hallway that opens right into the gourmet kitchen. The aroma of breakfast food and coffee fills the house.

Father's eyebrows are tight as he taps the screen of his smartphone. I walk around the kitchen's island to the large copper cappuccino machine and make myself a chai latté.

"Morning," he says, still looking at his phone.

"Morning." I sit at the table holding my wake-up juice, blowing across the top while warming my hands.

Overly happy, plump Mrs. Scott comes into the kitchen and retrieves a plate from the gas stove. She places it in front of me.

"You need a proper breakfast. Eat," she says in her laughably stern voice.

The plate contains scrambled eggs, bacon, and toast. More than my thin frame could eat, but my stomach betrays me at the sight of it.

"Thanks." I smile up at her, picking up the piece of toast.

"I can't believe you're almost done with school! Senior year, wow. Can you, Mr. Warrington? Growing up too fast." She touches my shoulder and turns away from the table.

"Um . . . yes, growing up," Dad says, too involved with some message on his phone. He snatches a piece of bacon from my plate.

Perfect, he's distracted.

"So, you don't mind about the back-to-school

senior camping trip this Saturday? I'll be there with Lucy and Emily. A group is going. We have our tent. I'll be home the next morning."

Still looking at his phone, he nods.

Excellent. Time to get out of dodge. I'm almost out of the kitchen when he speaks up.

"Is Daniel in the group?" He raises an eyebrow, taunting.

Shit. Here we go.

"He's a senior, yes."

His lips purse and his eyes drop to half-mast. The father-daughter stare down begins.

"All incoming seniors go. It's tradition to start off the new school year." I try to sound matter-of-fact, pulling the emotion from my instinct to whine.

"Let's see how this week goes. I may have a trip to New York and I don't want you there if I'm out of town."

"That's silly; you travel all the time. What makes this different?" I hold in my pissed-off voice. "Mrs. Scott is here and—"

"I'm sure Juliette, under normal circumstances, would be fine, but I'm the parent here, Willow. This isn't a school sponsored event, despite the tradition of it. I'm working on the details of my trip and hoping I don't need to go. Give it a couple of days."

I nod and put my cup in the sink. I spy Lucy pull into our driveway at the side of the house.

"Gotta run," I announce. I'm out the door, slinging my backpack over my shoulder and getting into Lucy's silver Audi Q3.

I smile a bit too broadly.

"He said yes!" Lucy squeals.

Laughing and taking my hairband from my wrist to pull my long dirty-blonde hair into a ponytail, I say, "No, but he didn't say no. It was better timing."

She takes off down the drive from my house. "I have a great feeling about this year."

I turn the radio up and smile at her. "You said that last year."

"But just think about it: we're outta here soon and going across the country to sunny Cali."

We drive out of the posh estate neighborhood with its perfectly spaced oak trees on either side of the street. It must have rained earlier this morning—the road is wet and the green lawns showcase wealthy manicured perfection.

We turn onto Pike Road, Lucy singing to the Twenty One Pilots tune "Stressed Out" and winking at me.

Yep, she's right; last year was good. All I'm hoping for is a quick year then onward to college, out from under my father's control. I can't wait. I already have early acceptance to Harvard, Columbia, and Stanford. My father is completely unaware of my applications outside of Harvard. Lucy is unaware of my acceptance to Columbia.

Lucy and I wait in the school parking lot until Emily pulls in and gets out of her sensible Camry, a car at odds with her personality. Her hair is messy like she just woke up, and her uniform is wrinkled, further complimenting her disheveled appearance.

Smiling wide and walking toward us, she calls out, "What up, my bitches?"

I laugh while Lucy cowers with a grin, afraid to notice who might have heard Emily. Probably everyone walking through the white stone archway of Trinity Cross that leads from the parking lot to the school grounds.

"Em, not funny. Let's not get kicked out our first day, okay?" Lucy turns to walk toward the entrance.

"Okay, mom," Emily pouts. She pushes her hand through her short-cropped auburn hair. It makes the left side stand up more than before. I point, and Emily does the maneuver again. This time, her hair seems to obey. "So, where is that heavenly mocha Marco at? With your handsome boy toy, Daniel?"

I shrug. "I guess in school already."

Marco is Daniel's best friend. He's the captain of the football team and very smart. He's at Trinity Cross on scholarship and everyone likes him—he has a smile that can win over almost anyone.

Daniel is laughing down the hallway with a group of friends. His eyes seek me out like he knows I'm near, spotting me in seconds. Daniel's tall, lean frame pushes off the wall of lockers with athletic grace and he comes toward me, Lucy, and Emily.

I can't help but grin at him. He returns his dimpled smile.

"So, we all have Mr. Brandt for homeroom." His arm casually hangs over my shoulder. He smells like a meadow on a spring day.

"Aren't you the lucky one," Lucy says. Emily

laughs, surprised at Lucy's uncommonly sassy comeback.

"You're rubbing off on her," Daniel says to Emily, wide-eyed.

Lucy blushes.

Mr. Brandt has us sit in order by last name, so naturally I'm in the back of the room. I like being in the back, out of the spotlight, with no eyes staring at the back of my head.

Mr. Brandt announces that as seniors, we are required to attend the morning assembly and to demonstrate the best that the school has to offer, which is code for being less goofy—especially the boys—and being quiet. We head to the auditorium and I sit next to Daniel.

Headmaster Chin starts by welcoming the freshmen and talks about the new open wing of the technology center. She reviews the academic code of the school and the rules of conduct. With few exceptions, the speech is full of all the same stuff as last year.

Walking out of the auditorium, we run into snobby, beyond-vain Coral Yang, Daniel's ex-girlfriend, as she waits with some of her cronies. She cues the fake smile and says hello to Daniel, all the while throwing visual daggers at me.

Ugh.

I don't like that Daniel is still friendly to her, but I try hard not to give Coral the satisfaction of showing it. I turn away while he continues to talk to her, still holding my hand. She laughs, which sounds more like a cackle. I could puke. Emily hooks my elbow, quickly turning me around and detaching me from Daniel.

Emily sings, "We're off to see the Wizard, the wonderful Wizard of Oz!" We skip forward. It seems perfect, since the Wicked Witch hovers behind us with Daniel. Gah, is it too much to ask that flawless Coral get a spontaneous nosebleed or trip over her own feet?

In the hallway, the bell rings to usher us all to our first period classes. I have Advanced English without my friends and walk away, spying Coral hugging Daniel. She stares right at me with a smug expression. A little nosebleed would indeed perfect her airbrush makeup. I huff and turn down the hall toward class.

Later, I have third period lunch and spy Marco at an empty round table. I plop down next to him with my tray.

"So, we've got the same lunch period," I say.

"Yeah, well, us brainiacs, ya know? Speaking of, where is Lucy? Isn't she in this lunch period?"

I look around. The cafeteria is buzzing, but no one new is entering. "She does. Maybe she ate and left already?"

Marco shrugs and takes a swig of his drink.

"How are your classes so far?" I ask, stabbing my fork through my salad.

"Good. It will be fluff all year, except for Mrs. Simpson's organic chem."

"Ugh, tell me." I roll my eyes. "I have that with you next class."

He laughs in his easy way. Marco has the charisma

that most guys want, he is dialed into school, and doesn't get roused up easily. Emily started to crush on him over the summer, which has resulted in some exciting flirting.

"So, what about—"

He interrupts me. "Nope, not talking about Emily, okay? We're all casual, and I've got enough on my plate." He laughs to himself and shakes his head.

I smile and finish off my salad and iced green tea. "Want to head over? Mrs. Simpson awaits to torture us with chemical madness."

We walk out of the cafeteria and down the hall. I look around for Lucy but she's nowhere to be found. Instead, Coral's cronies are huddled around some poor underclassmen, laughing and teasing her.

Marco catches their eye and winks at them. They smile and walk toward us. The girl slips away from continued torture as the bell rings.

"Nice job," I whisper to Marco. "I'll save you a seat." I leave just in time for him to be flanked by Team Bleach Blonde.

Marco slides into class as the final bell rings, grabbing the seat I saved him at the lab top bench.

"Cutting it close, Marco," Mrs. Simpson says.

"Oh, what I do to save those in need," Marco mutters under his breath with a grin.

Mrs. Simpson takes command of the class and starts in with a baseline quiz.

"Does this woman have no heart?" Marco asks.

"It doesn't count for anything, just a baseline of what we already know," I tell him. Although, I sympathize with Marco; who gives a quiz on day one?

The bell rings and I'm off to the technology center. I walk as quickly as I can past the plaque that proclaims "Warrington Hall." It's hard to be anonymous when your name is everywhere.

At the end of sixth period, the last class of the day, I meet up with Emily and Lucy at our lockers. They act as our central hub; we've had the same lockers since freshman year. Emily is laughing, but Lucy is wringing her hands and biting her lip.

"What up?" I open my locker to put in all the new textbooks I've been lugging around.

"You're gonna love it," Emily squeals with joy . She bounces up and down.

I laugh. "Oh, goody. Something happen to Coral?"

Emily nods.

"Wait, what?" My eyes grow wide as I look from Emily to Lucy.

Lucy is quiet compared to Emily's obvious excitement; whatever it is, it must be bad.

"Whoa, calm down Em. What happened?" I ask quietly. There are a few people looking over our way.

"It was epic! So, after assembly, I had World History with her, and she had this nosebleed. Nothing big, but like, it wouldn't stop. Tissue after tissue. She was wiping away her makeup with it, blood and foundation all mixed up—so gross. It got everywhere, and Ms. Johnston—old bottle glasses—was, like, blind to it. She told Coral to get a little princess grip and deal until after class, to go to the nurse. It was hilarious;

you should have seen the extravagant fit Coral was throwing. Then Lucy came in at the bell, and Coral ran into her and SPLAT! Coral, face-down, nose busted! Her skirt up over her ass." Emily giggles wide-eyed.

"Oh my god!" I breathe in disbelief.

"I think she chipped a tooth," Lucy says. "I was sent from the library during my free period to deliver a few books Ms. Johnston wanted.. I wasn't paying attention when we ran into each other. I feel horrible"

"Whatevs, you shouldn't. It was an accident. Coral is as mean as a rattlesnake. Happy to know she bleeds like the rest of us."

I can't believe it. Karma is on my side. "Did she go home?"

"Coast is clear. No more Coral sightings for the rest of the day. This is gonna be a great year, I sense it!"

"Ah, she was hurt, Em."

"I understand how awful it is that she was hurt, but the humiliation part she was due considering how she treats everyone she thinks is beneath her." Emily puts her hand on Lucy's shoulder and pats it. "I'm sure Coral will divert it all to her advantage soon anyway."

Lucy's eyes are cast down to the ground as we exit the school. My phone sounds with a text from Daniel: he has football practice and will call me later. I beam, getting into Lucy's car.

In the driveway at my house I try to reassure Lucy that Coral will be fine, but her mood stays the same. I climb out of the car, she turns up her stereo and heads back down the driveway. She must be worried about a Coral repercussion. She's famous for them. I should know—I spent most of last year experiencing them when Daniel and I started dating.

CHAPTER 3

It's three in the afternoon and I have an hour and a half before my appointment with Dr. Evan. So, like most well adjusted academic kids, I decide to goof off and grab a snack and watch TV. Duke and I take our usual spot in the living room. I'm sipping my Coke and noshing on kettle chips when I hear the back door. Duke perks up and then lays back down on my feet.

"Mrs. Scott?" I ask

"Just us," Mrs. Scott replies.

I get up to help and see Chef with Mrs. Scott, both carrying bags. "What's going on?"

"Special dinner tonight. Didn't I tell you that this morning?" Mrs. Scott starts putting items away in the pantry. Her hair is messy and she is looking and counting items frantically.

"No, I don't remember. Who is coming over?"

"A family dinner meeting of some sort; your father has requested you join." Mrs. Scott waves me off as she organizes items from the bags to the counter and puts some in the pantry.

"I have my doctor's appointment until 6 and was hoping to hang out with Daniel later," I whine.

Gah, let me find a way out of this.

I try to get more information out of Mrs. Scott, which reveals nothing because she doesn't know anything more. Finally, I leave, hanging on the word "family." It's an odd thing for her to say for just me and my father. I don't have much time to ponder the thought as I get ready for my appointment.

At the office, I hit the button that announces I'm at the door. The receptionist isn't at her desk to notice me and let me in. Instead, Dr. Evan walks over and hits the button himself.

"Sorry about that. Heather is out sick today," he says. A couple walks out as I walk in, smiling and holding hands. Wow, couples counseling and they are smiling? Okay, maybe Dr. Evan isn't a quack after all.

The office is quiet and I follow him to his office at the end of the hallway. He opens the door and gestures me to the chaise lounge, then goes to his desk to retrieve a notebook and pen. I realize he has several files on his desk, and he closes one.

"So, how was the first day of senior year?" he asks.

"Good. Typical, and some returned karma."

"How so?"

I shouldn't have opened with that. Counselors and their probing questions can't just let a dog lie. "This girl, Coral. Well, she's Daniel's ex-girlfriend. She's nasty to everyone, sits on a high throne. She got knocked down a peg today with an accident. What's interesting is I was thinking about this accident, and karma delivered, so yay universe!" I pump my arm in a small gesture, then immediately feel wrong. I'm a horrible person.

He leans forward, looking more serious than before. "So, you thought of what should happen, and it happened as you pictured it?"

Ice-breaking playtime over.

"Kinda." I avoid his eyes and tuck my legs under so I'm sitting cross-legged on the chaise. "I just saw her hugging Daniel, and she was giving me this smug look, so I briefly thought, 'It would be great if she got a nosebleed.' An innocent thought, right?"

"A nosebleed?"

"Well, the way my friend described the scene, it wasn't a simple nosebleed. She ran out of class, then ran into another person and fell, possibly chipped a tooth in the process."

Why was I feeling bad about this? I didn't physically do anything here. All I did was think about a nosebleed and about her tripping over her own feet. I shake my head.

"Coral had a rough day, by the sound of it." Evan's lips curve upward.

I nod.

"Tell me, were you happy about Coral's accident? Don't you find it interesting that you thought something and it happened?"

Where is this going? "It's just a coincidence. Coral isn't just mean to me and my friends. She and her crew are nasty to everyone. Everyone who she deems beneath her. I hate that."

"So, a core value for you is battling inequality?"

"Yes, of course. In this day in age, why wouldn't it be?" I ask.

He changes the topic. "It's interesting that your coincidences are a trending theme. In Dr. Bauche's notes, you wanted to hurt the boy who attacked you. You wanted to break his arm and throw him backward. It all happened. The fire was something you envisioned as well."

"No, no, this is completely different," I stammer. "I was overwhelmed with adrenaline and I was able to break free. I can't help his arm broke. It was at a funny angle; I'm guessing the way I turned put pressure on to break it when he fell and tried to catch himself. He was taunting me saying I wanted him while he was grabbing me, asking if I was scared. And the fire wasn't me at all! There were trash cans around that were burning. He knocked them over. I was in a bad part of town and it—there were homeless around. I think someone helped me."

"Why were you in Boston, Willow?"

"I got turned around. We just moved to Chepstow, and I was there with Mrs. Scott, shopping. We were going to meet at this one store. I dunno, it was all just messed up." I hesitate.

"Do you blame Mrs. Scott?"

I untuck my legs and stand. "No! Why would you say that?" I feel the heat of my face. Mrs. Scott called the police, she took me to the hospital and she cared for me. Father came when he could—a day later—but she was there for me and held me when I cried and babbled.

"She wasn't there to help you when you needed her in that alley." Dr. Evan stands up and places his notebook on the desk, then ushers me back to the chaise. I hesitate before sitting. "I'm simply curious as to your thoughts on this. How you ended up alone. How you ended up in that alley. How you got away relatively unharmed, but your attacker was hospital-ized with multiple injuries."

My thoughts? *My* thoughts?!

"I'll tell you what, that jackoff was telling the court he was trying to help me when I attacked him! He tried to turn it all around. He's the one with a record of assault, and he was blackmailing my father with his lies." I'm breathing faster. I know that if I don't retain control of my breath, the threatening tears will fall.

Breathe, Willow. Breathe.

"I don't want to argue over this. It's over. Why can't the past be the past and we just move forward?" I wrap my arms around myself and lean back into the chaise, closing my eyes.

"The 'why' is that you refuse to acknowledge the past and how it affects who you are. You block it as a self-protection mechanism, even though it is not protecting you at all."

"I don't know what you mean."

"Willow . . ." Dr. Evan pushes his hand through his hair. "Your accident with your mother. You blame your-self when, by all accounts, it was purely a car accident which you survived and your mother did not. In fact, she most likely saved you by getting you out of that car. You blame yourself for the attack in the alley and talk about how your father came to your aid with the plea deal to make it all go away. Again, not your fault. You protected yourself and got carried away at the closed proceedings that prompted this therapy." He pulls something from his pocket that catches the light and shines a moment before his hand cups it from view."Your blame is misplaced, and you will continue to have hard situations come your way that you will need to navigate through without self-sabotage. This is why regressive therapy is a good option, but you have to be open to it."

My collar is wet. I touch my cheek; my face is wet too. Shit, I'm crying.

"You're angry, and rightly so. You need to be able to release this anger and not implode."

This is a first. Dr. Bauche wanted me to adjust the focus on the positive, the future, blah blah blah.

"What, like take martial arts or something?" I shrug.

"Sure, or something." Dr. Evan's eyes shimmer.

I avert my eyes because I don't want to acknowledge my struggle versus how casually he sits in the chair across from the chaise.

"Willow?" He smiles. "You're more capable than you know. Deep down, you have a magick inside that you've tucked away. That needs release. It's a connection to who you are and what you are capable of."

Dr. Evan is now sitting next to me.

"What, like yin and yang?"

He nods. "How about we start this session? Are you open to this?"

I scoot back so my back is flush with the chaise. "I dunno. I have to be back for a family dinner thing. Will this be longer than our scheduled time?" I spy the small clock on the side table next to his chair and see I have less than half an hour left.

Dr. Evan's face changes. He is no longer sympathetic; instead, he almost looks angry.

"What do I have to do?" I stare down at my feet.

"You need to be open-minded and I will put you under hypnosis. Your subconscious will walk you through the past for you to understand those events better."

"Will it hurt?" I ask.

"No, not at all quite the opposite. Typically, you'll feel refreshed afterward."

"My father is aware, you said?"

He nods in confirmation. The idea of going back to my mother's accident weighs heavy in my heart. I want the ability to see and be with her again, but the cost is temporary and will surely haunt me. I miss her so much that it overrides my fear.

"Okay, then let's start."

Dr. Evan stands up and open's his hand , then pushes his chair closer to the chaise. I put my hands under my legs to steady myself. He's rocking a flower pendant in his hand and holds its chain loosely. Looking closely, I realize it isn't a flower; it's an intricate design of wrapping loops and circles. It seems oddly familiar.

"What is this design?" I ask.

"A triquetra, the balance of the mind, body, and spirit. A Celtic symbol."

I repeat "triquetra" and feel a tingle in my leg as if falling asleep. I squirm to adjust how I'm sitting. The chaise is firm but I'm able to gain some purchase of my position to snuggle in it better.

He begins swinging the pendant. It shimmers under the lights and follows the path of its curving design, where the three petal-like patterns intersect and are connected by a circle.

"I want you to listen carefully to my voice and relax, Willow. This is a place of safety."

My shoulders dip and my body sways. I follow the silver pendant swing back and forth, back and forth.

"Count with me—"

"One, two, three, four . . ."

CHAPTER 4

Back at home, I sit in the kitchen nook holding my warm cup of tea. Staring out the windows, I'm at ease, but sad for some reason. How can you be sad about something you can't remember?

I can't recount what I said during hypnosis with Dr. Evan; he said it was common. But I should feel a sense of clarity over the next day. He gave me his personal cell number should I have any questions. When I asked him what I said, he wasn't straight with me, and I knew it. He asked for patience and said we'd talk more when I could recall for myself more.

Has he worked with many teenagers? Seriously? Asking for patience when I wasn't all hip to this idea in the first place?!

The back door slams and I jump in my seat. Mrs. Scott is standing there.

"Sorry, didn't mean to scare you." Mrs. Scott hurries by me and heads for the pantry on the other side of the kitchen. "Why don't you go ahead and clean up? The company will be here shortly."

"Who is coming over?" I ask. "Come on, spill."

"Your father didn't say. I think some distant family member. I get the impression he was surprised, since we didn't have the event in our calendar." She pops a cashew in her mouth from the bowl I set on the counter.

"Is he home from the office?" I ask.

"He's on his way; he had a late afternoon meeting." She takes off her apron and hangs it on a hook inside the pantry door. "You know your father, always working."

I eat some of the trail mix from the bowl, then head up the back stairs to my room. My door is ajar, and I push it open to find Duke sleeping on my bed.

"Duke, you do realize you have your own bed, right?"

He lifts his head and starts to stretch.

My cell phone buzzes in my backpack and Duke is up and out of my room by the time I retrieve my phone.

Deserter.

I have several texts. I click on Daniel's first.

Sr camp trip? Didn't get to talk about it tday. Headin to work will call tnight.

I text him back to fill him in, then end with a kiss emoji that has me smiling as I hit send. Why do silly yellow pictures of facial expressions give so much extra meaning?

The other text is from Lucy:

Sorry about this afternoon. It was just Em, getting on my nerves. I don't like seeing anyone hurt, even if it is Coral. Gah, shoot me.

I get it. You have to admit Coral's a bitch... oops, I meant Karma.

LOL, let's hope it gives me some slack.

Stop worrying.

A moment later, the FaceTime app on my phone pops up with Lucy's grin. Lucy is sitting at her desk in the corner of her room by all her books. They're piled up from the floor like the Eiffel Tower. "Okay, I'm done sulking. What's going on?"

I tell her about the mysterious dinner that I need to get ready for.

Lucy's eyes open wide. "What are you going to wear?"

I smirk. "Are you Emily?"

Lucy belts loud laughter. Soon I'm laughing with her. Stress bounces off us both. When we finally stop and hang up, I immediately fret about what to wear wishing we had settled that question.

A closet full of clothes is daunting when you're not sure what to wear; everything seems wrong. Do I dress up for family? The safe bet, I decide, is to put on a pair of nondescript black pants and a sweater set. At my dresser, I finish up my routine. I brush my long dark blonde hair and tuck it behind my ear. The last accessory I add are my earrings, simple pearls with diamond points that were my mother's.

When I'm done, I'm out the door, heading to the beige and maroon abyss of the designer house. The decorator decided the accent color would be maroon, to represent my father's commanding place in the world. Of course, over time, I noticed her eyes lingered on my father whenever she was over. Thank god, I was able to divert her decorating eyes from my room, where I worked with Mrs. Scott to have bright colors everywhere.

I walk down the hallway, trying to hurry. When you're situated at the back of a 10,000-square foot house, it's difficult to go anywhere quickly. I round the large staircase that gets me to the front of the house. My father is there talking to a woman.

I stop in my tracks, and a vision of her crying flashes before my eyes. It's gone in an instant.

Do I recognize her?

Her long red hair waves as she turns, and she puts her hands to her mouth. I start down the stairs toward them tentatively.

My father comes to the stairs. "I would like to introduce you to your . . ."

She walks toward me, meeting me at the end of the stairs. Her eyes are glistening with tears. "I'm your grandmother. Sabine MacKinnon."

She is familiar, but she doesn't look like my mother, whose maiden name was MacKinnon. Mother was blonde and I'm more like her than Sabine with her bright red hair. She doesn't seem much older than my father, not nearly old enough to be my grandmother. I realize I'm assessing her and haven't come off the stairs yet. I step forward to shake her hand but instead get pulled into a hug. It is awkward and familiar.

"I've waited so long, and I'm so sorry," she says in a whisper.

Why is my heart beating so fast? I can't comprehend that my grandmother is hugging me. I thought she had disowned me, but the details are fuzzy. Father always clams up when I ask innocent questions about my mother's family over the years, so I dropped it. It wasn't like anyone from mother's side of the family ever reached out to me.

Sabine lets go and I move back from her awkward embrace, but she keeps her hands on my forearms. "You look just like our Nuala. Oh, Willow, I'm so happy to finally be back in your life."

I glance at my father, who is tense and standing like an oak tree in the foyer.

"Back in my life?"

Mrs. Scott appears and purses her lips as if she ate a sour grape. "Ahem, dinner is ready." My father escorts Sabine to the formal dining room. There is an extra place setting.

"Is someone else joining us?" I ask my father in a tone that is a little more accusatory than I intended.

He sits down while watching Sabine take her seat.

She lowers her eyes. "I'm sorry to say that, no, it's just me this evening." She places her hands on her lap and studies me with dark eyes full of sorrow. "Your grandfather, my husband, Harkin, recently passed away. He wanted to be here. I like to think he is, in some way, here in spirit."

Sitting next to her, I want to reach out and touch her shoulder or hand, but I don't know her. The sadness, that she wears on her face is genuine. "I'm sorry for your loss."

It was my loss too, for a grandfather I'd never known, already gone. I guess that's true for many in my family; my father's mother died when he was young too. His father passed when my father became an adult before I was born. I've never had relationships with grandparents.

"I have something for you." Sabine reaches into her flowing skirt pocket and pulls out a rectangular velvet-covered box. "It was your mother's. I wanted to make sure you had it."

My father's smile is constrained as he nods to me.

"Thank you, Sabine."

I take the small box and open it slowly. The necklace that lays within is similar to what Dr. Evan used in our session, only a little different with more loops. I've seen this necklace before.

"A triquetra," I whisper.

Sabine corrects me: "The pentacle of the Goddess."

I touch the pendant and it shimmers under my touch to various colors.

"That's a rare type of opal—"

Sabine stands up, interrupting my father, and

reaches out. "Let's try it on. Your mother wore this as a teenager. It seems fitting."

I smile at her, thinking about my mother and how I miss her. My fingers lightly brush over the necklace, its smooth stone embedded in silver. When I glance at my father he seems off. He has a scowl on his face from being interrupted by Sabine.

Mrs. Scott brings the first course to the table and I take a sip of the soup. Happily, I taste a simple mushroom broth.

The silence is like a fog settling in for the long haul. I break the tension by asking, "So, has this dinner been planned for a while?" I ask my father.

He scoffs sarcastically with a sideways glance toward Sabine, "No, not really. I'm afraid that my input to this evening is as a bystander, regardless that I'm the head of this household."

"Aiden, you can't keep Willow hidden from us any longer." Her voice rises as if she holds authority over my father. It's impressive since so few do.

"I don't understand," I say to him, then look back at Sabine. "I thought it was your decision that you didn't want me around, because of the accident that killed her." My voice shakes.

"What? No. No, that's not true at all—"

"Sabine!" my father exhales. "Willow, I have had rules about the association with your mother's family since the accident to keep you safe. It was agreed to, not only by me."

"Why? Why would you do that? Why would you only tell me now?"

The next course is brought in, and my anger at my father mounts. I had always thought that they chose not to be in my life because I was in part to blame for an accident I don't remember. One of the deep scars I carry.

A vision flashes before me—my mother and me in an upside-down car. She is hanging by the seat belt, her hair like a mop in front of her face. I move from the back seat and start to shake her. "Mommy." My voice as a little girl pleads to get her attention. Someone grabs me and pulls me out of the car and I scream and yell when my mother reaches for me.

I blink several times and the image is gone. I'm no longer in the car, I'm back at home in the formal dining room. My vision refocuses on my father. He stares back with pinched lips and waits for Mrs. Scott to exit the dining room.

"You're angry."

"Damn right," I snap. "You've been hiding things from me, lying to me!" I scoot from my chair and he rises from his.

"I need a minute." I walk to the washroom out in the hallway and shut myself inside.

Looking at myself in the mirror, I shake my head. "Okay. You've been lied to. Long lost relatives. No big deal. Control the controllable. I can learn." I shrug and wash my hands. The tingle of the water is icy and cools my hands and thoughts. When I turn off the water and leave the washroom, I can hear them talking.

"Can't you sense the change in the air? Her

binding will not last long. The tide of change is here, Aiden, regardless if either of you is ready."

"We have time. This was not a good idea, you coming tonight. I'm not sure how she's going to react. There are others here to protect her. You're entitled motives do not override the fact—"

Sabine laughs sarcastically. "She can protect herself if you allow her too. You can't keep this tucked away and run off again. I can feel it. Surely you can too? Me being here is not the trigger, it's already happened."

Then they both spot me standing in the open archway to the formal dining room. "What are you talking about? And before you say 'Nothing,' " I say, pointing my finger toward my father, "neither of you are quiet speakers."

Sabine smirks while my father stares at me with a clinched jaw. He is ready to ground me for life. I never speak to him or guests disrespectfully, but tonight my tongue and brain don't seem to have any restraints.

"Willow, you are royalty," he announces.

I double over and laugh, my hands shaking and static electricity runs across my fingertips. The tingle in my arms ignites the familiar feeling from Dr. Evan's office.

I spy Sabine's wide-eyed grin, as I shake my hands free of the sensation.

"This is a joke, right? I mean, come on, there isn't real royalty anymore. I've been going to school like any normal kid."

Okay, normal wealthy kid. Let's be fair, here.

"You're descended from an ancient line of druids and Wiccans. And with Harkin's passing—your grandfather—the crown belongs to you." Sabine clasps her hands together. She's . . . hopeful?

I sit down, processing what she just said. Pause, rewind, and play again. Is this a joke?

She's serious and it looks as if she is holding her breath. I'm angry, but good grief, she doesn't know me and she just came in and dropped a bomb.

My father sits back in his chair and observes me. I hate that—the parenting tactic of sit and listen. What's the right reaction here? The long-lost grandmother is speaking of craziness, royalty, and witches. Why is everyone calm?

"Let me get this right: you're here because I'm the next in line for some crown that I never even knew of, and I'm from a line of witches?"

My eyebrow shoots up and I withhold my verbal doubt out of respect for a lady who obviously believes this deep down. I glance over at my father for some kind of interruption, but his jaw is firm, his eyes steady.

I huff at them both and wiggle my fingers in the air. "So I have some kind of magick, then?" As the words leave my lips, the electric tingle runs across my fingers again and a faint blue light appears on my skin. I shut my hand and it disappears.

What the hell?

"What do you call that then?" My grandmother gestures toward my hand, eyebrows raised. "Static electricity?"

I wave my hand accusatorially. "Static electricity does not equal whatever craziness this is!" I say, frustrated.

She grins at my father. "See? Are you going to deny her? Unbind her at once!"

My father leans forward and unleashes his deep commanding voice. "Sabine, you have no authority here. This is my daughter and you came here to trigger an event. It isn't all about you and your political power trips. Are you scared she might deny you?" He pushes back and stands from the table to continue his rant.

Mrs. Scott is walking down the hall and, upon seeing my father, turns right around.

This is ludicrous. What is she talking about, unbinding me? What's he accusing her of?

There's a flash. I shield my eyes. Then the light is gone.

I'm in the dark woods with my mother. She is touching my small face. Her familiar dark blonde hair reaches her shoulders in waves. Her blue eyes sparkle and her smile is reassuring. Her hands are touching me, warm, soft, and loving.

"Stay here, sweetheart. It will be okay."

I nod.

I blink and my eyes are swelling with tears. I just heard my mother's voice! I haven't seen or heard her since that night. I had forgotten her voice. Air catches in my throat.

There is another flash and I'm back in the dining room no longer that little girl in front of her mother.

I fidget in my seat, then stand, overwhelmed. The uncontrollable part of me is building. I shake all over. A loud hum sounds all over my body.

"Willow." My father brings my attention back to him. "As strange as it sounds, everything you are doubting is true, from magick to royalty. After the accident, I used magick to take away your memories of that horrific event. I also removed your memory of our heritage and extended family as a safety precaution."

I listen to what my dad is saying. I'm his little girl, caught in his shadow, hoping to make him proud and awaiting his grin of approval. This time, however, all I can do is gape at him while tears escape my eyes.

My voice shakes. "Is that what Sabine is talking about—unbinding? I'm . . . bound?"

He's standing in front of me. "Yes," he replies, reaching for me.

I move away from the table and from him. "Don't! I don't want to be unbound then."

Sabine's mouth hinges open.

"I don't want what you're saying! Keep it. I don't have to accept it, do I?" I'm still shaking. I clasp my hands into fists at my sides to steady myself. My mother—I miss her. I want to listen to her voice again. None of this changes anything.

My father's eyes are wide and his forehead creases. "No, you don't. But your magick will beat on the surface and build. Your mother and I are from particular family bloodlines, and your choices will be irrelevant. Magick will come."

Irrelevant? No choice. *No choice.* The words ring over and over in my head. My father and Sabine are talking to me, moving toward me, but I can't understand them. My anger builds—the static electricity moves over my body and down my arms, filling my clutched hands with zaps of pain.

No choice.

No choice.

No choice.

I'm shaking more now, and the electricity is compounding. It shocks my arms hard. It hurts, but I bear the pain of stabbing needles into my skin. In all this chaos and confusion, the pain at least is known and something real.

Sabine is no longer moving toward me but retreating.

She should. She brought it.

Her fault.

No choice.

My vision lands on my dad, my father—the man who lied to me. Protected me. Kept me in the dark. Loved and provided for me. His hands are up and he is chanting something, his eyes fill with tears.

Crying? That's not like my dad. Oh, this is bad.

The detachment, the unbinding, it hurts—it's as if it's ripping my soul.

"Wil-low!" My mother's voice calls out, but she isn't here. I look for her but my eyes show me someone other than my mother. Someone I don't know, but yet he feels familiar. The energy is all around me, consuming and drowning. I suck in more air to breathe, then release.

My scream reverberates through the house.

The dining room bows and the windows shatter as I fall to the floor. My dad catches me.

Darkness engulfs me.

CHAPTER 5

Cold, crisp, artificial air blows on my arms. I'm struggling to wake up fully when I hear, "Okay, Sleeping Beauty, time to rise and shine before the warden makes her way in here."

I open my eyes slowly and see the white walls and beige tile surroundings. Emily is sitting across from me in a twin bed, dressed in jeans and a plain white T-shirt. Her short-cropped hair is messy, as usual.

"Where are we?" I ask, sitting up. My eyes still refuse to completely work. I rub them and focus more on Emily.

She gives me a funny smirk. Before she can answer, there's a knock at the door and Dr. Bauche enters the room. She tucks her shoulder-length wavy hair behind her ear. Her composure is graceful as she stands at the end of the room in front of the window. The soft light surrounds her in an ethereal effect that has me tongue-tied.

"How are you feeling today, Willow?" she asks.

Emily announces her departure and is out the door before I can exhale. I watch her leave and want to go with my friend. What am I doing here in the first place? Why would Emily be here?

As if reading my mind, Dr. Bauche says, "Willow, we've been through this before. You've been here before." She taps on an iPad and scrolls. "I'm more concerned about the outburst at dinner."

Dinner? I don't . . . I shuffle back toward the headboard of the bed I'm sitting in. It suddenly floods my brain—dinner.

Sabine.

Magick.

Royalty.

A vision flashes before me of Sabine crying and hugging me. She is dressed all in black and she tells me how much she loves me. We are at a funeral—my mother's funeral, I realize, because my arm is in a cast. How can I have forgotten Sabine at my mother's funeral? I'm not here though, I'm somewhere else. I shake my head to clear it and I'm back in the small white room.

Dr. Bauche's demeanor changes as she sits down on the bed next to me. The springs of the mattress squeak under the new weight.

"You had an outburst that wasn't coherent. The staff last night had to sedate you. Instead of placing you in confinement, I recommended shared quarters."

She waits for me, but all I can do is stare at my

hands, remembering a blue light, thinking about my mother's funeral and meeting her mother, my grandmother. She continues, "Something about a grandmother and Wicca?"

Did she just read my mind? I survey the room, stalling. Oh, no—it's what I always dreaded. I'm at a psych treatment center. How did Emily end up here too? She wasn't there at dinner. I remember the hypnosis with Dr. Evan. It must be what's causing visions.

"Is Dr. Evan here?"

Her eyes search me over in an evaluating way that makes me uncomfortable. She must notice.

"I don't know a Dr. Evan. Is he your internist?"

I stammer my words, confused. "No, no. I started seeing him a few weeks back at your practice. He's a new doctor." I need him to help explain this—the visions that keep popping up and the regressive treatment therapy. I don't need to be in a treatment center.

"Willow, we can meet at our regular session time today. I'm not aware of any Dr. Evan." She stands. "You can go to group, but first take your meds." She hands me a small paper cup with three pills in it.

I consider the cup and then her. She nods to the sink, toward a drinking glass.

"What are these for?"

"I need you to take them, Willow, as part of your therapy regime while you're here."

I stand and walk toward the sink hesitantly,

thinking about how not to take the pills. That regression therapy, last night . . . I'm not taking these pills, who knows what they will do to me. She watches me take the pills and drink the water. I have to show her my open mouth and move my tongue to show I'm not holding pills hostage.

Where's the trust?

I grip the pills in my left hand, where I slipped them next to my water glass. Score.

Dr. Bauche quietly leaves, satisfied.

I study the pills in my hand and decide to keep them. I open a door next to Emily's bed to find a full bathroom. I walk back to my side and open another door to find a closet with clothes and shoes. My clothes are recognizable, especially my favorite hoodie. I put the pills in a hidden pocket in the sleeve. Then I get refreshed and open the door to a bare white hallway. I feel like an escapee, but I'm lost. I need an exit sign.

There's laughing at my left and I walk to a room labeled "Yellow Brick Road." Several teens are lounging around on beanbags, sofa sectionals, and floor pods. I see Emily in the far corner. A counselor acknowledges me and waves me in. I sit by Emily.

"We need to talk," I whisper to her.

"This is some crazy." She is distracted, looking at a guy sitting across the room in ripped jeans and a black T-shirt with a gray hoodie. His long, messy hair falls forward on his face and his arms are folded. He appears asleep until he speaks. His voice is soothing and deep.

"I'm not going to talk today, so let's move it along," he says.

The guy running the group replies, "Theon, this is not going to move you forward on an outpatient basis. You have to put in the work."

Theon settles back in his beanbag chair, and the counselor turns his stool to me.

"So, Willow, did you find your triggering point?"

Emily is staring at Theon, smiling. Most in the room are paying attention to other things besides me, except the counselor.

"My triggering point? I don't really—"

"From yesterday's activities? I observed the trigger with your family. There is anger. A lot of anger."

The counselor mentioning my family and accusing me of anger heats up my face. I don't know who he is and how he knows anything about me or my family, despite him talking as if I do.

"Sure, I think most teens will say they're angry—it's not unique."

A few kids sitting to my left affirm my statement. Emily half-heartedly laughs.

"Yes, that is certainly true in the general sense," the counselor says. "However, none of you are here in the general sense. Actions intended to hurt either yourself or others have brought you here. Your time here is to teach you how to control those triggers and behaviors."

I take a sharp inhale. Did I hurt someone? No. No, I couldn't have—could I?

Emily leans forward. "Those actions make me, me!

Are you trying to change me, Brad?" She drags out his name mockingly.

He smiles, unmoved by the outburst.

"No, not change in the sense you're assuming, but I do want you to become aware of your impact on yourself and your surroundings."

Flipping her hand dismissively at him, she says, "I'm totally aware."

Theon stands up with small grin that barely shows under all his hair. Two bumps on the top of his head are just visible beneath his hoodie.

"Theon, ready to share?"

"Uh, no, it's time to go," he says in his smooth voice.

"Ah, lunchtime," Brad confirms, looking like he's happy too.

Everyone stands up and leaves the room. I walk with Emily down the hallway.

"What is going on?" I ask.

"I'm not sure, but it's your party, so I'm just along for the ride." She claps me on the back.

"My party?"

We turn the corner and follow the line that enters a small cafeteria. Emily stops me and guides me to an open door on the left, a storage closet.

"Listen, we can continue to play psychoanalysis rehab if you want, or you can get on with it."

What the hell is she talking about? I'm in the process of asking when she holds her hand up and cuts me off.

Her eyes are staring directly into mine. "You're

tougher than you think, or we wouldn't be such close friends. You need to snap out of it, Will." She snaps her fingers. "You, me—we don't belong here in your head." She lightly touches my temple.

"My head?"

"Ask yourself why you'd have me here, besides the fact that I'm awesome. I do what?" Her eyebrow raises.

I search and say the obvious response: "Tell it like it is?"

She nods.

Ding ding ding. I'll winning the fair prize if I can just complete the puzzle.

"Why would I—"

"Don't focus on the 'why,' focus on the 'get-out-of-your-way' task. You think too hard and long about stuff, and sometimes you just gotta do and move forward." She scans around real quick and adds, "Although you did do a great job bringing that demon, Theon, here. At least it was worth my time."

How did I bring or do any of this?

She's becoming translucent. I reach to touch her hand, and she chuckles at me as my hand passes through hers. I'm starting to fade along with everything else in my head.

"Bravo, Wills. See you soon," Emily whispers.

Before I can process it further, I'm gone and laying in my bed at home.

I grab my phone and text Emily.

I just had the strangest dream and you were in it.

I wait despite the late hour, hoping she might respond.

Yep, I'm so dreamable. Go back to sleep girl, you're interrupting my beauty sleep.

Chuckling at Emily, I put my phone down and close my eyes.

CHAPTER 6

"Willow, sweetheart, wake up."

The bed dips as my father sits down. I'm home. Something about that word—home—warms my insides. Home can mean different things, but for me in this moment it is stability, a constant, and, in my changing world, a necessity.

I blink at the bright light, remembering my weird dream with Emily. My father turns off the lamp on my nightstand. I must have left it on.

"Hey. You're home?" I ask, slowly sitting up.

"Of course I am. Do you remember last night?"

I sit up and see he's in casual clothes: jeans and a long-sleeved, dark green shirt.

"Yes, I do. Is Sabine still here?" I rub my eyes of sleep.

"No, just us. Mrs. Scott is out today; she'll be back this evening. Let's take the time to talk."

"What about school and—"

"I already spoke to Lucy and the school." He swallows and stares at his hands. "I want to spend time with you and answer your questions about magick, along with the whole royal succession that is expected of you—and there is an anticipation of your —coronation."

I can't help but cringe at the word "coronation." Me, a girl who trips up the stairs on a regular basis—a girl who understands nothing about how to preside or rule, or whatever the heck it is all about—Queen?

Is this something I really have to do?

I want to go back to sleep and just veg out and forget all of this. I can't though; I recognize the hum of the magick in my veins now.

Duke pushes his nose in through the open door and jumps up on my bed. His tail wags and both my father and I pet him, as if the silent moment we share will be one of the last normal things we do.

He breaks the silence in a soft, unassuming voice. "Come down when you're ready. Mrs. Scott made French toast that I'm sure even I can reheat."

He leaves and slowly closes the door.

Duke licks my face and lays his head in my lap. When I touch my face, the tears flow as if from a hose down my face. Gah. I'm not usually such a crier, but I'm a cry-baby now.

I waggle Duke's ears, wipe my face dry, and get dressed in my comfy clothes. Duke leads the way to the kitchen.

I'm greeted with almost the typical scene, except father isn't on his cell tapping or talking. He's staring out the window, holding a cup of coffee. He appears older to me. His dark brown hair is brushed back, revealing glints of silver at his temples. His square jaw is taut. I don't want to interfere his thoughts, so I stand in silence.

Duke gives us away when he barks.

"I'll feed him if you can heat up Mrs. Scott's delicious French toast," I say.

Duke bounces up and down when I pour the kibble in his bowl. His happiness changes my solemn mood.

The plates are at the table, garnished with strawberries for flair and two slices of bacon. The syrup sits in the middle of the table. My father is staring at the cappuccino machine with his forehead creased.

"Need help with that?" I ask.

"If you want your tea, absolutely! This takes high skill." He laughs.

I lift the lever into my cup to steam the milk, adding my tea to finish it off. Then we head to the table.

We eat in silence for a long while before I break the tension.

"So, you grew up and always had powers?"

I still can't believe this. Here I am asking my father about magick and powers. I pinch my leg just to make sure I'm not dreaming still.

Damn it—it hurts. This isn't a dream.

Taking his last drink of coffee, he answers, "Yes, I grew up with magick, although my powers were bound until I was older. This is the case for most families where powers are anticipated. Powers vary for

Wiccans and can depend on bloodlines. For our family, specifically, you will be envied by many." He pauses, frowning. "Actually, by most, which is dangerous."

"Why is that dangerous?"

He stares out the bay window. "It's dangerous because of my bloodline—and your mother's. Nuala's bloodline is royal and is of pure white magick, whereas mine, although a noble bloodline, is full of dark magick. Our union was not sanctioned. Nuala was next in line for the crown. Her older brother, Liam, renounced himself from the family and died young. Her younger brother, well . . . he passed away when you were little. The MacKinnons' royal legacy boils down to you."

His expression is pensive. I don't want to talk about mother and death; I want to focus on something light.

"Rebel. You and mother ran away, then?"

He grins and laughs. His eyes light up at the thought of my mother. "We did. We got married and pregnant with you within a year. The best year of our lives. But Harkin, your grandfather, and the Guardians caught up with us. When we went back to face punishment because we went against your grandfather's wishes, it was more of a celebration that you were with us. Not all was forgiven, but your mother was next in line for the crown, so she committed to the duty."

"So she would have been Queen?"

He nods.

"But the accident . . . changed everything." I breathe in the weight of my words.

So much for something light and easy to talk about. That accident has been the reason for so much change in my life and our family. I can't look at him directly, so I look out the bay window and hug my knees to my chest.

When I glance back at him, his eyes are gray and sad.

"After the accident I met with Sabine and Harkin, and we made a pact to protect you. We've moved around to keep you safe. There are many in Edayri that believe there should be a sovereign government over a royal one. We didn't believe the accident was just an accident. We all knew that, in time, you would need to ascend the throne following Nuala. Your mother was the white light in my darkness, just as you are. She was brave and smart, and ready to change the times—which, unfortunately, I'm sure others didn't agree with. Harkin and the Guardians worked hard to learn all they could about the accident, but unfortunately, all I can tell you is that demons were involved."

"Demons?" My mind reels. "So, what types of magickal beings are in this place that you call a realm?" I'm not sure I really want him to answer me.

"Every kind you can imagine, and some you may never have heard of. The big five are Wiccans, demons, valkyrie, fae, and shape shifters."

"No vampires? You know, the kind that sparkle?" I giggle to myself, thinking, Go Team Edward!

This is all absolutely nutso. The smug smirk on my

father's face doesn't gel with my sense of humor at that moment. Seriously though, fae and shape shifters? I don't even know what a valkyrie is, but this is just—

Watching my father, my lightness is shattered. It's all I can do to keep my chin up and stare at him—my father, a dark magick Wiccan. A man who is formal and overly organized, a man who is usually in a suit and tie in some board meeting. This man has magick at his fingertips, and now I do too.

"I'm sure there are, but I doubt they sparkle. You need to take this seriously, Willow."

I lean back in my chair and look him in the eyes. "I am taking this seriously. I didn't mean to offend, but this is a lot to take in. I don't want to be the whiny teenager throwing a fit, but my world is rocked, and a little levity every now and then is okay . . . right?"

I cringe, hoping he doesn't jump down my throat. He doesn't, and that's worse.

"I do forget how young you are." He gathers his dishes and mine and goes to the sink. I follow him to his office, and we sit in the maroon wingback leather chairs that face each other in front of the fireplace. I tuck my left leg under my right leg. I'm waiting, not sure what to say, what to ask. What I can handle. I think learning everything in the full rush last night broke me somehow; I'm timid. I don't want to break —I don't want to have an episode and wake up again. Besides, it has been a while since we've sat and talked at any length about something important and meaningful.

My father opens his palm and a blue light dances around his fingertips. It's like the light I saw in and around my hands last night. My eyes follow the wave of light. I can't help but be amazed. It's like nothing I've ever seen before in real life; magicians on TV have got nothing on this. It is seductive and intimidating, and I can't help but feel cool that I have it too. This whole magick thing is unwanted, but at the same time, maybe—

My trance is interrupted when he says, "You are unique when it comes to our family's powers. You embody both the light and the dark. I like to think Nuala is more prevalent in you than I am, but the fact is that you have more dark magick. You should know it's taken me decades to learn that magick is magick, no matter where its base form comes from. Dark doesn't necessarily mean bad, just as light doesn't necessarily mean good."

"What does it mean, exactly?"

"The power derived from you is as individual as you are. I leaned full into what I needed to accomplish in order for the power to carry out what I needed it to, which some label dark magick. Your mother, on the other hand, leaned more toward what something should be, like a remedy, again, to which some would label as white magick."

He closes his palm and the dancing blue light extinguishes immediately.

Frowning, I ask, "Do others believe that dark magick is wrong?" The word "dark" worries me. Will it change me? And if my power is as individual as I am, who am I?

"Willow, there is a lot of prejudice within magickal families. I think you would use the terms 'snobby' and 'over-privileged brats.' Whether it be light, dark, or anything in-between, they will measure magick in percentages like DNA. For Wiccan culture, it's about purity above all and one with nature, the Goddess, and the spirit. It's not that different with other magickal beings."

"So, they're behind the times it sounds like. Joy."

"In many ways, yes," he replies. My sarcasm is not bothering him.

"How am I going to learn everything? I know nothing about—what's it called? Edayri? Or about who lives there. I'm an outsider. I can't imagine anyone will be thrilled with me showing up. If I don't accept the crown, what will happen?"

I really hope he answers with "No big deal" or "Democracy wins out."

"A little chaos will ensue."

Of course. I sigh and lean back in my chair.

"But the biggest impact would be to those of the previous crown. Legend has it that the family's blood-line magick can be reversed. I doubt it's true, but the belief is that once things are undone, the space-time continuum in which we live will change and revert, ripping. A rift. Who knows? The point is, no one has seen it, so we can't predict exactly what would happen. I'm sure you've heard the saying 'magick comes with a price'?"

I nod; every movie or TV show that has witches notes it as some moral aspect. I guess there may be a few Wiccans in the entertainment business. Hopefully I'm not as far behind in learning as I thought I was.

He continues. "The same goes for the royal position. There is a price for each judgment, each sentence, and each law. The idea is that this balances out the power of the position to limit the person who holds the crown, and their family."

"Okay. Interesting."

My father stands up and walks to the fireplace, where he pulls a hidden lever. I never noticed it before. The bookcase rocks backward, revealing a dark passageway. I stand in awe. He walks in and, with a wave of his hand, the entryway lights up.

I follow him, remembering to close my gaping mouth. This is wild; my house has a secret room!

The room is painted dark green. Shelves of books adorn one wall and an oversized, puffy, paisley-patterned loveseat acts as the only casual seating. There's a table like the one in my chemistry class, with a sink and burners in the corner with a cauldron. A fireplace shares the wall with my father's office. The room looks like just the place I'd want to hang out in with tea and a good book.

"What is this?" I ask.

"I guess you could call this my lair. Or you can just

call it my private coven, since I'm a singular practice witch."

My father's eyes twinkle with excitement and his whole demeanor changes like he's an excited kid at Christmas. I can't help but mirror him. The father before me is so different from twenty-four hours ago. I wonder if he sees me the same way.

"What do you do here?" I gesture to the cauldron and the bookshelves that house a few glass bottles with stoppers. "Do you practice magick or make potions down here?"

"Truth?"

I roll my eyes. "Yes, truth. It should be an open book."

His smile reaches his eyes. I haven't seen that since I was a little girl. It's like I have my daddy back. I suddenly want to do anything to keep him happy.

"Speaking of books," he says, pulling a thick one from the shelf, "this book not only contains all our ancestry information, but also magick incantations, potions, and fortunes."

"Fortunes?"

His smile broadens. "Your mother really liked that toy—the magick eight ball—so she developed a spell and added it to be a part of the Book of Shadows to make it a fortune teller. Although I suspect it only tells you what you are ready to know, sometimes it's good to have the confirmation."

"That is so cool!"

My father shows me the book. Flipping through, I find that several places throughout are blank. He explains that only family can read the book, and it will only show each individual what they need to see. This book is especially unique because my father and mother incanted their separate family's books into this one. It's not that old, but it possesses centuries and centuries of information. He shows me how to get into the hidden room and how to leave it. He then leaves me alone in the room with the Book of Shadows for most of the afternoon.

I think about my most basic question. "Show me how magick was started."

I flip through the book the way my father showed me and the scrolling script appears. I learn that divinity revolves around a goddess and a horned god. I read further that the pentagram is an elegant expression of the golden ratio phi which connects to ideal beauty to express trust about hidden nature. I always thought the pentagram was an evil symbol, but now I want to see if it would show Coral's hidden nature to Daniel and the school. I laugh to myself at the thought.

I keep reading and am surprised how connected Wiccans are to nature and the flow of the spirit. There are many elements to which Wiccans ascribe physical power; however, the element of the spirit is the most coveted, as it's balanced with all the elements—air, water, earth, and fire.

As I read, I lose any sense of doubt. The pages are filled with stories and facts about my heritage and my family's history, and I no longer feel like it is just me, father, and Mrs. Scott anymore.

That evening, Mrs. Scott joins us and we eat dinner together. She's a practicing Wiccan but is limited in physical powers. Her own identity doesn't come as a surprise since I knew she helped raise my father when she was much younger.

"Oh, my Willow, your father was a mess when his binding was removed. A complete mess—it was like a poltergeist was living in the house, mind you. He went through a time where he could hardly reach for something without it flying across the room. He stunk for a week—the water wouldn't stick to him to clean him!"

Listening to Mrs. Scott tell these tales about my father makes me roar with laughter. It's nice to see he struggled too.

"Okay, okay. In my defense—ah, well, it takes some time is all."

Mrs. Scott continues to giggle and I take in the ease of my father's shoulders and manner. This is my family and I love them.

I'm happy Mrs. Scott knows about everything; it means I have someone else I can talk to. It's not like I will be able to share this with Lucy, Emily, or Daniel.

I practice my ability to control my power with my father. Mrs. Scott watches in awe and laughs and claps with joy after almost every exercise. My hands and fingers develop a white, lacy, flowing pattern, like henna, when I conjure my magick into a light-blue flame like my father's. The patterns on my hands and fingers disappear a few minutes after I let go of my magick.

I can feel the pull to do more, but it's getting late.

The day has gone by so fast. I've learned so much—from calling my magick to the surface to controlling my intent and use of it. Mrs. Scott pulls me into a bear hug that makes me feel like a tiny toddler, but I love it.

"Oh sweetheart, you will be the best for the all of Edayri." She kisses me on the forehead and I turn to my father as she leaves.

"Thank you for today," I say.

"I'm here for you, Willow. I love you very much. I know you have your doubts about all this, but Mrs. Scott is right—you have the makings of a fine queen."

My father walks up the stairs and I feel proud of myself. It's the relationship I've always wanted with him—what we did today, what we used to do when I was so much younger. I don't know what happened over the years, but I'm happy now, and now is what matters.

PART II

"Darkness is coming for you," Fate taunts.
The girl defiantly walks forward.

CHAPTER 7

Cabin fever is setting in; it's been three days since I've been to school. My father felt it was safer for me and my fellow classmates, now that my magick is unbound. Thank the heavens it's Saturday. He's back to work, although staying home as much as he can. I've been catching up on schoolwork and practicing my magick. Once I can prove my control, I can go back to school and see my friends. Mrs. Scott and I have been catching up on reality television in between all the work stuff. For some reason, she is fascinated with *The Bachelor* and *Housewives*.

The senior campout is tonight. Father has been putting protection spells on the property, but somehow, someway, I need to figure out how to escape the house. I miss my friends, and it could be one of the last things I'll get to do with them. I try not to think about this too much. Besides, Daniel and I've been texting and I really want to see him. I haven't reminded my father of the senior campout; why let him say no?

I enact my plan with counter spells I learned from The Book of Shadows, placing my heat signature on Duke. I will leave only with my clothes so as not to trigger the firing squad of alarms. I work on my homework because, according to the school, I'm only on leave until further notice due to a "family event." Like a private school really cares—especially when you're funding most of their projects and buildings.

9 p.m. and the time has come. I'm committed and going to the senior campout. I put on my favorite hoodie. I have Duke happy and content on my bed, and I turn on my computer and put on a music loop. My backpack in hand, I decide that sneaking out the back door is my best option. I call to my magick and have it surround me. I walk forward slowly and repeat in my mind, acceptance to pass the boundary without harm. When I'm at the yard's perimeter, I take a deep breath and step outside the spell protection borders.

I exhale. No alarms, no smoke, no fire. All clear.

Self-satisfaction beams out my body and I take off at a run to where Emily and Lucy are waiting for me.

Operation: Free Willow is a success!

Emily is jumping up and down and Lucy waits, smiling, in the car. Emily hugs me.

"Dang Wills, good to see you. I've been having wild dreams lately."

I smile at her. "You too, huh?" I probably shouldn't have told her all about it, but she seemed to think it was just some type of symbolism of my subconscious mind.

She laughs and we settle in the car. Emily parks her Camry on the north interior side of Salem Woods in one of the few parking spaces left. Lucy and I gather our gear from the trunk and hike into the clearing, guided by music and lots of laughter. You can't say private school kids don't know how to have fun, 'cause here we are, per a tradition that started long ago. Every year, class leaders apply with the park rangers for this weekend. It's all legit, although it still feels like we are rebels.

Oh, the privileged.

"Come on! You two are so slow!" Emily trots ahead with the tent on her back, slinging a small cooler in one hand and a bag in another. She doesn't seem bothered at all by the weight she is carrying.

Lucy laughs. "She'll trip soon, I swear, and then we'll catch up."

"She's definitely over-caffeinated tonight," I respond. I rearrange my hold on the bags of food and my backpack.

"I think it has more to do with Marco. He's more flirtatious than usual," Lucy says.

"Oh really?" I laugh easily. I missed the mundane gossip, and I really missed my friends. This is my joy.

Emily makes her way toward the other edge of the clearing, where a firepit is lit up with a crowd of students. I spy Daniel coming out of a nice-sized tent with Marco. He spots me, smiles, and waves. I wave back. He is handsome in flannel. I've never seen him in flannel before.

"You're so lucky," says Lucy.

I break my stare from Daniel.

"Why do you think I'm so lucky?"

Lucy nudges me with her shoulder as we keep walking. "Uh, one of the cutest, nicest, most all-American guys is, like, totally in love with you. Nope, not lucky at all. I take it back."

"Okay, hisso." I nudge her back.

Yeah, Daniel is great. It's funny, though. I would think most girls' parents would like Daniel, but for some reason, my father doesn't. At first I figured it was because he wasn't wealthy, but that idea was put to rest when Mrs. Scott informed me that he would be this way about anyone I was dating. I remember when I dated a boy named James in 8th grade who took me to a dance and kissed me on my front porch step. Father was grumpy about that too, so I guess it's just a father thing. Part of me likes his protective nature because it reminds me that he loves me.

We walk to our spot. Emily is already unpacking the tent. We all pitch in and get it up in under ten minutes. Fire pits glow all about the clearing—a large one near the concrete pavilion in the middle and several small ones around tent groups. The music is bumping at the front of the clearing, and set up in the middle by Steve Carlin's tent is a keg. Steve is the typical jock party boy, and friends with everyone, but too friendly with most of the girls.

As soon as the tent is up, Daniel grabs me by the hand and leads me to the side of his tent.

"Hey, you," he says, holding my face.

"Hey." My breath leaves me and my body tingles at his gentle, familiar touch.

He kisses me like he's starving and I respond, so eager to see him. It's familiar and electrifying—his touch, his kiss. Daniel makes my knees weak. I wrap my hands around his neck and pull him closer, and his hands have just dropped to my waist when we're interrupted by a high whistle. We turn to see Marco sporting a big grin on his face. Emily and Lucy are just ahead of him, walking toward the center pavilion.

"We're heading over. Come join us when you're . . . um . . . yeah. Finished." Marco laughs and turns to walk away.

Daniel is looking at my lips.

"Are we finished?" I whisper.

I feel like the air is gone from my lungs when he leans down and kisses me one more time, softly and sweetly.

His smirk catches me off guard as he pulls back slowly. "For now," he whispers.

Clasping hands, we round the tent and head over to chat with Steve and some of the others while enjoying our Solo cups filled with beer. Everyone is having an excellent time, laughing and carrying on about the upcoming school year. No one asks why I haven't been there. Everything is easy and fun.

Daniel has his arms around me. I love that he is taller than me and can hold me like this. Emily is off to the side, laughing and poking at Marco, who returns the favor.

"So, I hear Marco may finally return Emily's advances? Is that right?"

Daniel kisses me just under my ear. "Maybe, I dunno, but he'd be silly not to. They flirt like crazy. Might as well just get it together. Everyone thinks they're together anyway."

"Yeah, true."

I look for Lucy and spy her talking with Coral. Coral is a fashion model on a camping trip, dolled up ridiculously. If they walk over and she is in heels, I may hurl. They turn toward us moments later. I don't see any heels. I guess I get to save my vomit for another situation, and the awful beer might just do it. I dump my cup out on the ground.

"Hello, Daniel . . . and Willow." Coral says my name like it burns her mouth. Wouldn't that be nice? I notice her teeth seem to be fine, so either she's already fixed the imperfect chip that happened on the first day or she didn't chip a tooth after all.

"Hey," Daniel responds. His arms are still around me, and he kisses my neck again.

I try not to gloat on the outside, but on the inside, I'm full of in-your-face celebration. You're his ex, Coral. Stop trying to cause issues and throwing yourself at him, he's with me.

"Hello, Coral." I immediately look toward Lucy. "Hey, Lucy, we're gonna head back to the tents. Come over later and join us."

Yeah, Coral, you're not invited. Don't come, I

think to myself. She leaves and heads straight to Steve, who I'm sure will relieve her of any misgivings.

Daniel puts his arm around my shoulder and walks us back to the tents where our small fire pit is glowing. Both done with our Solo cups, Daniel tosses them into the fire where the plastic burns quickly and folds in on itself, producing gray smoke. It smells awful. The smoke curls and twists like an arm. I shake my head just as Lucy walks over with Marco and Emily, chatting away and laughing.

I scratch an itch on the back of my neck.

"The bugs, right?" Lucy says. "Don't worry, I've got a little sage stick that should solve the problem!" She dives into our tent and returns with a small bundle that she lights up. It starts to smoke white, and she whirls it around until Emily snatches it from her and starts dancing around the fire.

"Are you a witch, Lucy? Seriously, this is a witchy thing to do." Emily eyes her as she waves the smoke around. I sit up a little straighter in Daniel's lap.

"Are you okay?" Daniel asks me.

I nod. "Yeah, just adjusting." I snuggle back into Daniel, but all I can think about is the rehab dream and Emily's presence in it. I haven't talked to her about it beyond saying she was in my dream. Is it just a coincidence?

In any case, it sounds crazy to speak of a psych rehab unit and say, "Oh, by the way, you were there with me!" It's bad enough my BFFs know I go to a psychologist on a regular basis. Lucy says all the rich and famous do and that I shouldn't sweat it. I'm not the rich and famous type—or, at least, I try to reject that notion. I rub my hands up my arms and come to the secret pocket of my hoodie. It has something in it.

The pills from the dream. Shit. It was a dream, right? I pinch my arm and feel the pain. At least I know this is real.

It's well after midnight now. The music is dying down and those who aren't staying over in the camp are starting to leave. The crickets are getting quieter and the temperature is getting colder. I'm happy to have the extra blankets.

Emily and Marco shout in sync, "Ghost stories! Lucy, tell one!"

Lucy's face is flushed red. "What? Are you kidding me? I don't do ghost stories!"

Marco whines. "But you're the one who reads all the time. Come on! You've gotta tell us one."

"I've got an excellent story to tell." Emily gets very animated and lifts her arms toward the fire as if she is trying to make it rise.

"You know we are in Salem Woods. These are the very woods where several witches were burned at the stake. In their damnation, there were incantations uttered that continue to linger even to this day."

Marco laughs. "Em, seriously? We live here. All the stories we heard in elementary school and junior high are just whacked!"

She gets a serious look on her face. "I'm not kidding you. My stepbrother, Charlie, knew this girl. She was a grade older than him. She came out to these woods with a bunch of friends. They were hanging out having a good time together, not that different than tonight."

She waves her hands around and the fire seems to follow her movements as if she controls it. I tuck my arms into myself.

"Someone said a chant as a joke, and the next thing they knew this girl went comatose and started to float."

Daniel sits up and begins to tap his leg as if remembering something. "Oh yeah, my sister was just a grade under them at that time, and she remembers that story. I totally didn't believe her because she was always saying stupid stuff."

Emily continues. "Oh, it was real all right. Charlie knew her boyfriend. They were on the football team together. The boyfriend was devastated. The girl's parents blamed him and even took legal action against him and his family. She was admitted to a mental institution, and to this day she hasn't spoken or said a word."

Everyone is hanging on Emily's every word.

I wonder what would happen if I did something wrong tonight with my magick, not on purpose. I bite at a hangnail absently. Which of my friends would be pulled into my fate by accident? Father has taught me more control, but suddenly I'm filled with guilt. I'm out in the open for selfish reasons, and not only am I taking a risk, but I'm also taking a risk with my friends' wellbeing.

Damn it. I suck.

"Now, the wild part is this: last year a medium came to these woods. I remember Charlie said the family hired her to help their daughter." Em shakes her head to clear her thoughts. "The medium came to the woods and stayed here for hours, then retreated to town all upset. She said this girl, their daughter, was a payment to the debt owed."

"No," Lucy whispers, raising her hand to her mouth.

"Yes. The curse was lingering when it finally found a member of a family that it could take vengeance on. The saying goes, if you step in these woods, beware of the family toll."

Emily's voice drops. "The toll must be paid, Willow." She starts to rock back and forth with her knees tucked to her chest. She repeats "The toll must be paid" several times.

I'm stuck. I don't know what to do. Is she really possessed?

Daniel hugs me protectively. "Cut it out, Em."

Marco pushes her to the side and says, "Real funny."

I hold my breath. The air shifts, changes.

Emily breaks the silence, yelling, "Rrrahhh!" She jumps up and tags me on the shoulder.

"Gotcha!"

Everyone joins in laughing, but the air shift is still there. I smile and try to play along, but inside I'm falling apart. Emily is a joker, but what if I have a family toll too? I mean, we are Wiccans and my family has powers.

The air, the change in mood—someone is watching me. I feel that creepy, icy feeling tingling down my neck. I don't consider myself brave in the least, but I'm not going to let my friends or Daniel get hurt. My own lack of safety I can accept, but theirs? No way. I wish I could lay down some protective spells. I have no idea how to use spells yet.

"Hey, I'll be right back. I need to use the facilities," I announce.

Daniel grabs his flashlight. "I'll go with you."

"I can handle it," I say, taking the offered flashlight. "I'll be back in a few."

Daniel tries to change my mind and Lucy offers to come as well. They finally go back to the fire pit at my stubborn refusal. Out of all the tents in the clearing, only a few fire pits have teenagers around them anymore. It's gotten late and most are calling it a night.

The cold air licks at my face as I walk down the pathway and pass one of Coral's obviously tipsy cronies. A boy I don't recognize wobbles after her a minute later, reeking of beer. I tense seeing him, because he looks similar to the boy in the alley I've all but tried to forget. I shake my head to clear it and stumble as I reach the edge of the bathroom facility. The lights flicker and a vision flashes before my eyes. I reach out and the building I was near is no longer there.

I'm in the woods as a little girl in my pajamas and coat, holding my arm to my body. A deep voice calls me a little witch. It is taunting me when my father appears. He has blood all over him, but I'm not scared, only relieved. He swoops me up and we hug each other tightly. It's the accident all over again. I blink several times and the vision is gone, but my goosebumps remain.

The regressive therapy and hypnosis is making rethink my decision.

CHAPTER 8

I walk past the bathroom facility to the side of the clearing, just about twenty feet from our tents. I can somewhat make out my friends, and I wave to show I'm okay.

I'm not okay. What the hell am I doing? I wiggle my fingers to test my magick, but nothing happens. I flex my hand and try again. Still nothing. Clutching my hand to my side, I walk into the woods just beyond the trees. When I hear the earth give way to something off to my left, I ask meekly, "Who's there?" I don't recognize my own voice—I sound like a little girl.

No one responds.

"Who's there?" I say, louder this time. A rustling in the canopy of the trees is all that responds.

It could be an animal. Except if it is an animal, it's not a small one.

The sound is getting closer.

I turn back to the campsite, but all I see is the

forest. I went too far. I turn left, then right—my sense of direction is gone. How did I get this far into the woods?

What the hell am I doing out here? I clench my hand and feel nothing. No light, no magick.

Pop.

Snap.

Tree branches are breaking.

I'm out of time. Someone or something is coming toward me!

I jog forward. There is a faint light on my right and I head for it. Then I hear it.

The voice is deep, full of menace. "Little witch."

I freeze.

"Little witch, come play with me. I promise not to kill you quickly. That way we can both enjoy it."

My mind is locked up but my body is moving of its own accord now, running in the opposite direction of the baritone voice. I'm clumsy and scrape against rough, unfriendly trees and bushes. I flex my hand but there's still no magick. Whoever's chasing me huffs through his nose like an animal. A breeze licks at my neck and I feel my insides go cold. I'm in that alleyway in Boston, with the boy touching me and taunting me. I can't breathe.

The glowing light on my right is getting brighter, calling to me, as if it will help me get away from the threat. It's fight-or-flight time. I won't be a victim who waits. On shaky legs, I run at full speed through a break in the trees.

There is the anguished cry of an animal behind

me. I run as fast as I can without tripping on the uneven forest floor. My heart is pounding. I can't see well and my breathing is labored. I don't seem to be gaining any distance toward the light. I pump my arms harder.

He's gaining on me.

Smack.

Something hits me in my shoulder and I'm on the ground.

"Aaaahhh!" The pain sears like a hot iron.

Shit!

I know I've been stabbed with something, but if I lay here in pain, I'm dead. I know it.

No time.

No time.

Keep moving.

I scramble to my feet and turn, only to find myself facing my attacker.

Death has come for me. He's real—a dark-skinned skyscraper with massive horns that rise above his head like a bull's and long claws sharp as knives. I am terrified and mesmerized by his red glowing eyes like something straight from Hell. His powerful muscles ripple. This could be a scene from a movie, though nothing that I have ever seen.

He's real. This is freaking real.

He stops in front of me, smirking. "Little witch doesn't know how to play yet. I see."

His fangs show white against his dark skin. I notice that his belt is laden with various types of knives and other weapons. Favoring my injured left shoulder, I scoot away from him. I've got to get away.

"This isn't as satisfying as I had hoped, but your heart will taste good either way!"

He lunges for me. I roll my body and push my knee off the ground to jump into a run.

I'm dead for sure if I can't move. As I pop up, the unbelievable happens! A ball of white light passes me and hits Death's chest and throws him back against a tree. He's down.

Scrambling, I turn to run, but halt as I find myself face-to-face with a warrior. He's in dark and sleek full-body armor. Have I seen him before? He is the most gorgeous guy I have ever set eyes on, with wavy hair and assessing eyes. I go from full-on flight mode to completely stunned. I can't move.

His commanding voice is but a whisper. "Stay quiet and hide."

I nod, wince and touch my bloody, throbbing shoulder. Something is stuck in it—a knife, a branch, a freaking Mack truck, I don't know! The pain pulses all over my back and side. I try to control my breathing so that it's quiet, but I'm starting to shake. I have no control. I hope this warrior is a good guy who doesn't want me equally dead or I'm in big trouble.

Death laughs.

"Ah, the Guardian Captain comes to protect his little witchy queen wannabe, does he? Finally, an opponent worth my time!" The creature huffs again and again, as if smelling the air.

The gorgeous guy vanishes from my side. I hide behind the brush next to some trees and hug my knees to be as small as possible without causing more pain in my shoulder and back. I close my eyes. I try to slow my breath to find my magick. Where the hell is it? Pain overrides everything. I tug on my hoodie's zipper; my cotton shirt is sticky with sweat. I touch my shoulder and it feels wet—blood.

Smash!

The loud crash is followed by a tree falling next to me and I nearly scream. A white ball of light illuminates the forest. Then I hear the clanging of metal. Swords? Someone falls hard.

I ready myself to run.

"You can come out now, Willow."

He knows my name?

I slowly stand, my fear abated, then bend forward just as quickly. I wobble. Blood pools down my side. My shirt is soaked. I walk over to the animal-death-creep thing and kick him in the groin.

"Asshole!" I yell. My bloody hand starts to light up with the scrolling design. Geez, finally!

In his unconsciousness, he takes it like most men and curls to the side.

The gorgeous guy smirks. "Um . . . okay then." Shaking his finger at the creature, he says, "No children, Tertium."

"Tertium? This thing has a name? You know him?" I take a small step back, holding my left arm steady.

His head tilts to the side. "Yes, by reputation only.

He's not a 'thing,' he's a demon blood warrior." He says this like it's a well-known fact.

I shake my head, not believing what just happened.

"For simplicity, he's an assassin. Although not a very good one." He kicks at the demon's feet. Then he throws a stone to the ground, which unfolds and grows four times its size, focusing light on Tertium.

Tertium opens his eyes and stares at me. "More will come. Your father will pay too, little witch. The demons will feast on his heart for all the glorious dark—"

Suddenly he's gone. The light shrinks back to its small stone shape.

My gorgeous hero sticks out his hand. "Enough of the mysterious. I'm Rhydian. Your father sent me to watch over you."

Watch over me? Rhydian doesn't look that much older than me. Wow, that face. I clear my thoughts and gesture to where Tertium just vanished. "Thank you for that."

"Yeah. Tertium isn't much of a threat. All bark, not much bite. Whoa!" He winces at me and points to my shoulder.

"It's bad, isn't it? It freakin' hurts like nothing I've ever felt before." Although the pain is starting to fade, so is my vision and balance. I think I might pass out.

He stands behind me. He moves my hair to the side and is touching my back, looking at my wound. I can barely feel him there, just the throbbing.

"It's gonna hurt for a second, but I can heal you quickly enough. Ready?"

Hell no!

"Okay," I say in an exhale, and hold on to a tree partly to brace myself and partly to stand. A moment later my back and shoulder erupt in sharp pain and I scream, white knuckling on the tree.

Then Rhydian's hand is pushing into my wound and soothing warmth takes over, followed by tingling. The iron smell of blood is overwhelmed with the smell of antiseptic. It feels like my muscles are stitching back together. The pain is gone, as if novocain has been rubbed inside all over. I straighten and wipe my face of tears and possible snot. A few moments ago I survived my first assassination attempt; now I'm sure I look like a blubbering mess.

"You did well. It's healed," Rhydian says.

Facing him, I feel embarrassed for some reason. Surely a warrior like him sees these kinds of wounds all the time.

"Thank you."

"Of course." A push of a button on his wrist band seems to disintegrate his armor before my eyes, revealing his regular clothes. He wears dark jeans and a gray long sleeve shirt that hugs his biceps and lean frame. He looks like a college student, maybe in his early twenties. His hazel eyes have specks of yellow in them.

I feel strangely at ease with him, but I don't think I know him. I can't stop staring.

"Have we met before?" I ask.

"I know your father, Aiden—Mr. Warrington. He and my family are friends. I'm a Guardian assigned to you for your protection." His friendly smile is off-putting only because it makes him even more attractive. "I don't think we've formally met until today."

A little creepy. If only his face and those eyes weren't so damn—

Okay, focus. My father.

"Does he know I'm here?" I snap unexpectedly. Did he send this guy to drag me home since I wasn't supposed to leave the house?

"I haven't spoken to him in several days." His brow creases in concern. "I should give him a call about what just happened."

"He doesn't know I'm here!" I shout out. "Rhydian, right?" He nods to confirm that I have his name right. "You don't need to—"

I can hear the faint calling of my friends. They sound worried. "Willow, where are you? Willow?"

How the hell am I going to explain this? I look down at my bloody shirt, then up at Rhydian and across the flattened forest. I sigh in defeat.

Tertium would have been easier to explain if he wasn't trapped inside a stone.

Emily runs through the trees in front of us, looking determined. She slides to a halt, looking directly at Rhydian with her eyes squinted.

He grabs me in a quick movement as she steps forward, standing tall, then unexpectedly waves and blows me a kiss.

What the crazy hell?

Awkward. It's like she knows something that I don't. Like that dream in the psych rehab facility . . .

For a nanosecond, Emily's in front of us, and then she's not. I feel a change of footing and I stumble backward. Rhydian is holding me from behind protectively. It feels too intimate, too close, and I try to put space between our bodies.

A whirlwind of force pushes me forward and backward, but he holds me steady. The world has gone blurry and I can't see anything solid, just whites and grays smeared together in a fog. Time is folding in on itself, in on me, and outward, the pull-push sensation of weightlessness. I lean forward and my feet are on solid ground again. I feel the immediate absence of Rhydian's arms and body.

We are no longer in the forest. Instead, I'm in a room surrounded by large men.

CHAPTER 9

Where the heck am I? The three men around Rhydian and me are intimidating, muscled, and tall. One even has bruised knuckles. I step backward, away from them, only to run into another. Are these friendlies? They look to be about Rhydian's age.

"Okay, guys, back off. Give her a little space," says Rhydian.

One of the men points to my side, where my hoodie is stained with blood. "Were you in a battle? Is she hurt?" His hair is dark and curly.

Rhydian explains what happened and that he healed me. They seem to relax, and the one with bruised knuckles turns around and sits in a La-Z-Boy chair. I realize that I'm in a living room of some kind —a cabin room judging from the log walls. A small fire in the fireplace gives off light and heat. It's the only thing comforting and familiar in the room.

I turn to Rhydian. "Where are we? Who are these guys?"

All except the one in the La-Z-Boy chair smile at me. His dark menacing glare seems concentrated directly at me.

"Guardians," Rhydian says in a low voice.

"Oh. Hello." All return the greeting except, again, the one in the La-Z-Boy. He seems to be sizing me up.

"How about we get you cleaned up," Rhydian says. He guides me just outside of the room to a staircase. I don't know why I'm blindly following him, except that if he wanted me dead, he could have killed me back in the woods. He made it sound like he was assigned by my father to watch me, and I believe that —it totally sounds like my over-protective father.

We turn right at the top of the stairs. I yawn, covering my mouth. There are closed doors on each side of the hall. He opens one and I walk in. He points to another closed door. "The bathroom is in there."

"Thank you."

"Shirts and clothes are in the dresser over there. Feel free to use this room if you want to lay down or anything. I'll be downstairs."

"Can't you just take me home?" I ask.

Rhydian glances at the floor. "No. I have instructions to keep you away."

"Instructions?" My voice hitches.

He's still avoiding my eyes.

"Why? What is going on?"

He doesn't answer right away. I go to the bathroom and splash water on my face, cooling the anger that is building up inside me. Patting my face dry, I turn toward the bedroom. Rhydian is sitting on the bed.

"We're off-grid," he says. "Your father and mine think there's a coup of some kind going on at the High Coven. As soon as the coast is clear, I'll deliver you to your father."

"He didn't tell me any of this." I pull the hair tie from my wrist and put my hair up, trying to take in everything that Rhydian said. I unzip my hoodie and take it off, looking it over. It's completely ruined. My shirt looks even worse. Pulling open the dresser drawer, I find a small stack of T-shirts. I grab the black one on top and walk to the bathroom to slip it on.

"When did you talk to my father last?" I ask from the bathroom.

"It was my father who contacted me when I was on my way to find you."

The shirt is three sizes too big. I gather it on the side and tie a knot so it fits better. Rhydian stares at me when I walk out, eyes wide and assessing.

"I need to call my friends and let them know I'm okay," I say. "I totally disappeared on them; they probably called the police." I pace the room thinking about Daniel and about Emily's strange reaction to seeing me. Oh god, how am I going to explain any of this to them?

Rhydian steps in front of me, stopping me from pacing. "Tell me how you know a valkyrie. I saw her acknowledge you."

I start to chuckle, but his eyes are serious. "You

mean Emily? She's been my friend for over three years. She's just Emily. What's a valkyrie?"

"The valkyrie choose heroic slain warriors to become immortal as einherjar and fight under valkyrie command. They've been around forever, originally from the Norse plane before it was destroyed. Typically, seeing a valkyrie means death," Rhydian says, his brows raised.

I almost didn't see the La-Z-Boy Guardian in the doorway, his dark clothes and skin, blended in the dark hallway, his eyebrows also raised at me.

"What?" I challenge him.

"So, your best buddy is a valkyrie, eh?" His accent sounds Irish. "Ya know, valkyrie are a rare female warrior breed and they're the best in all of Edayri. So you might wanna recheck that friendship, 'cause if push comes to shove, she's gonna choose her blooded over the likes of a Wiccan—especially a royal." He spits the last part like it tastes bad in his mouth.

"And who are you?" I spit back. He is immediately not my favorite. Apparently this Guardian is judging me, so I might as well return the favor.

He huffs and throws his hand in the air in frustration, turning around. "Food is ready," he says as he walks away.

My stomach growls at the mention of food. I follow Rhydian back downstairs to an open kitchen and hearth.

"Let me introduce everyone to you, Willow," Rhydian says. "Cross, you've met—excellent in battle strategy and fighting, and pissing people off."

Cross shoots Rhydian a squinted stare, but he ignores him and continues.

"On your right is Quinn, our resident medic, IT wizard, and typical geek." Quinn nods distractedly at me. "And this is Tullen. He's our historian and religious conscience."

Tullen has a different appearance from the others, with strawberry blond hair pulled up in a man bun and a beard in a bright shade of red. Everyone else is clean-shaven with short hair.

Rhydian and Quinn seem to be the youngest in the group, although not by much.

There's not much pretense when Cross brings the food to the table. They all dig in quickly. I follow suite as my stomach betrays me with a loud growl.

After we eat, Tullen smiles at me. Cross still looks irritated with his pinched lips and squinting eyes. Quinn leaves the room, calling someone on his cell phone.

I break the silence. "Can you let me text my friends? I understand we can't go back but they are probably freaking out."

Rhydian shakes his head. "That isn't a good idea."

"Why? Lucy will call the police." I remember he knows nothing of my life, my friends. "She's one of my best friends. You haven't met her, but you saw Emily before you—by the way, how did we get here?"

"Transporting magick," he says matter-of-factly.

Tullen taps his wristband; it's the same one Rhydian is wearing. It occurs to me that they all have the same wristband.

Nothing good will come from me disappearing.

"It's dangerous," Rhydian says, answering my first question. "Your magick is unbound and more will be hunting for you. Before you take the crown at the winter solstice, you're fair game."

"For what, exactly?"

"Changing of the guard—taking over the crown. It would raise a li'l chaos. All are eager to take yer blood magick." Cross's eyebrows are taut and he takes a drink of coffee.

"I don't understand what you're talking about," I reply, confused.

Tullen says, "You have to die for your magick to be released. If it goes to the void, no biggie, but if someone incorporates it into themselves, it becomes their magick."

I bite my lip, contemplating that. He means the demons are coming for me.

Tullen gets my attention. "Hey, I don't mean to scare you. Do you know much about Edayri? The realm in general?"

Cross chuckles. "Hell, no she doesn't. She's what Quinn calls a noob."

"You're what I call an asshole," I respond matter-of-factly to Cross.

He seems to relish my retort. Tullen gets up and, grinning, pats Cross on the back. Rhydian tries to hide his amusement but smiles unsuccessfully. I haven't done anything to warrant Cross's smart-ass attitude, but I'm not going to be intimidated by him. He seems to acknowledge this; his dark brown eyes crinkle at the sides with a smirk. He likes to push, and I will push back.

"Basically, you're a pure source of magick and all the crazies are gonna want a taste," Tullen says from the kitchen. "Most Wiccans and beings have limited magick and physical powers, even the noble and the High Coven."

Rhydian chimes in. "Guardians, too. We have some physical magick, but these"—he points to the wrist band—"amplify our magick among other things."

I recall Rhydian in his dark armor in the woods. The back of my neck tingles as I think about seeing him for the first time. Right before he saved me from the blood warrior demon.

I really am a noob to this world.

Quinn comes bounding into the kitchen. "Rhy, Eoin has discovered us missing and he's on the trail. They know Willow is out and has been located."

"Shit," Cross grumbles.

"He's calling out for information on us too. He's pissed."

"Who is Eoin?" I ask.

"Eoin, is the head of the Guardians, the commander," Rhydian replies. "I guess you could say we are rogue for the moment."

I listen to them, feeling guilty. I'm the reason these guys are in trouble. Rhydian says that my physical signature would be tracked back home and to my friends. He and Cross discuss their next move to take me somewhere else.

"If they don't find me, will they hurt my friends or my father?" I ask.

"Depends on who 'they' are. A fae isn't too vicious, but depending on the demon and how upset they are at your blood, they could take out their anger on someone," Tullen responds.

I stand up, alarmed. "I gotta go."

"To where? We're rogue; our ability to help is limited. I swore an oath to protect you. Your father will be all right."

Cross chuckles sarcastically at Rhydian's comment.

Rhydian ignores him. "I'll go check the campsite if that will make you feel better."

"Can I borrow a cell and just text my friends?"

"Bad idea. Then the bad guy sees who to torture to get ya to come out," Cross says.

What the hell! This is insane!

Quinn's arms reach out to steady him; from what, I couldn't see. "Did you sense it?" he asks Rhydian and Cross.

They nod. Then a shock wave goes through my body. I must look surprised because Cross makes a comment about me feeling it too. "It's the rift," Tullen explains. "It occurs when the Edayri realm portals are split between planes."

"The British are coming," Cross says, looking around like someone might come through the wall.

There's a shock wave again, although this one makes me step back to steady myself and lasts longer.

Tullen and Quinn touch their wrist bands, which

immediately turn to liquid metal to cover their bodies. It works so quickly that if I didn't see it happen, I wouldn't have believed it. Everyone is suited up in sleek dark armor.

"That was the fourth movement," Quinn says.

"Ladies, we're going to have company. We need to move!" Cross has a wide grin and his eyes sparkle, like a dog getting a treat.

The rogue Guardians leave the kitchen one by one and move downstairs. Rhydian and I follow them into an empty concrete basement.

"Have you used your magick before?" Rhydian asks.

"Yes," I say in a whisper. "I'm not well in control yet, but I'm working on it." I don't know why I need to say that to Rhydian. I feel like such an outsider with them.

Tullen asks, "Do you have it in your mind?" He gestures to the rogue Guardians.

"What?" I ask.

Rhydian nudges me and whispers, "Don't worry, I'll transport us together. We need to move to another safe house." His armor is similar to the others' but fits him differently and there's an insignia on his pectoral similar to the Goddess's symbol on my mother's necklace.

"How do I transport?"

The guys all blur out, one by one.

"Visualize where you need to go," Rhydian says. "It's like folding into yourself and folding out where you need to be."

It sounds crazy, but it's my only shot at getting back home to my friends. *I can do this*, I think, trying to build up my mental confidence.

Rhydian reaches for my hand, and I close my eyes and visualize the foyer of my home. I feel my body vibrate and allow the flowing movement to envelope me.

I hear Rhydian yell "No!" When I open my eyes he blurs away, reaching for me. As I pull away from him, my vision clears. I'm in the foyer of my house. I did it!

CHAPTER 10

I t's early in the morning and the house is empty and dark. I can barely make out the grandfather clock down the hall near the formal dining room. The sconces in the entryway flicker with faux light, and I can see the table in the middle of the foyer. I open and close my eyes. Everything is black and white like a noir film.

This isn't right.

The entry light turns on and blinds me. When I refocus my eyes, nothing has changed; my vision is still without technicolor.

"Hello? Willow? Mr. Warrington?" Mrs. Scott is in her robe, her hair still messy from sleep. Her plump frame and cheery face are a welcome sight. She shuffles in her house shoes and tugs at the lapel on her robe.

"Mrs. Scott."

She looks right at me and again says, "Hello?

Who's here?" She is biting her lip and shivering. She can't see me. I get right in front of her and wave my hands in front of her face, but there's no reaction.

"I know someone is in here. You'd better leave if you know what's good for you," she warns.

She must be able to feel me there but not see me. I'm just happy to see her. I want to hug her, not only to comfort her but myself as well. I need to lean into her pillowy body with her sweet, flowery scent. I need my family—her, my father. To understand what's going on and how Rhydian fits into the mix. Is he someone I can trust?

"Something is wrong," Mrs. Scott whispers. "I feel it." She turns away from me and walks to the front door slowly.

"I'm here!" I try to get her attention but it's useless. She can't see me. I'm caught in some kind of in-between from transporting wrong. I'm not really in her presence but I can see her. Rhydian warned me and I ignored him; I have no idea how to get out of this. I try to transport again by myself, concentrating on the foyer of my house, but I don't move.

A loud noise from outside shakes the house. The furniture moves and the hanging lights wave in warning. Something else is here. I exhale to control my breath. If I get scared like before, my magick will be of no use to anyone.

Bam!

"Oh goddess," Mrs. Scott says, clutching the lapel of her robe and shuffling backward toward the foyer table.

The front double doors fly open and she's flung back to the wall near the sitting room as if pushed by an invisible force. Something flies up the stairs, leaving only a trail of gray smoke. A large, horned demon with dark red skin walks in followed by three people in cloaks.

Mrs. Scott screams and holds up her hands in surrender.

My power is pulsing on the surface of my skin, but no one can see me. Will my magick even work if I'm not truly there?

I throw a light ball at the group coming in the open door. It goes through them like it was never there.

A cloaked figure floats through me and comes to stand in front of the red-skinned demon who resembles the devil similar to the demon from the woods who stabbed me in the shoulder. He's not the same, yet I feel the phantom pain in my shoulder. The familiar hum of my magick is gone.

"Father, help! Help her!" I scan the room to see if anyone hears me, but the group in front of me seems unaware. I yell again. "Please, Daddy!" I hold myself and hold my breath.

"Neither the girl nor Aiden is here. It's strange because I sense the girl. Maybe she left recently?" The voice coming from the purple cloak is female.

The demon huffs and smells the air. In a deep timbered voice, he says, "You're right, it's strong in this room." He focuses his yellow eyes on Mrs. Scott. "Where are they?"

I can see Mrs. Scott shake and I ache for her. He stands menacingly in front of her and touches her face with a clawed finger. She turns her face to the side. He will hurt her—his intention is clear to me. All I can see is the boy in the alley, the demon from the woods, and now this red devil hurting the kindest woman in the world. The woman who raised me and is not only family but my confident, my friend, and my surrogate mother.

I run and step in front of her. My magick swirls in my hands. "I'm right here! Don't you fucking touch her!" I scream, my vision blurry.

"Will you be cooperative or suffer the consequences?" he taunts.

No! No, no, no, this can't be happening.

"You will not take the crown. It isn't yours," Mrs. Scott says with a shaky voice. He leans over her. I try to touch her but my hand goes through her shoulder. It's as if I'm a ghost in this room. My voice hitches in my throat as I say her name again like a silent prayer for help.

Does she know I'm here?

"Oh? How do you know it's not already been taken? These are all just formalities at this point. The plot is enacted; your little girl will be but a casualty." He sneers, fangs showing.

"I'm okay! Mrs. Scott, please, please run—"

Mrs. Scott moves away from the wall and speaks to the one in the cloak standing amongst the other demons, their face hidden from view. "I see you. You should be ashamed," she says. "The Goddess most certainly is. You have denounced her and this chosen royal family." Tears spill down her chubby cheeks.

"Do it," says the lady in the purple cloak before she turns and floats out the front door.

My anger is at this demon in front of me. I know what he intends to do. I throw my conjured offensive magick light balls at him with absolutely no effect. I'm screaming and yelling. My arms are lighting up in the scrolling patterns of my magick, the design expanding from my hands to my wrists, elbows, upper arms, and shoulders.

She holds her hands up and there is a small glow of light. I try to add to it, to give her my magick—

Thud.

The demon is sheathing his bloody sword with an indifferent face.

I can't move.

I can't turn around.

I just keep throwing the light balls and trying everything I can to make them count. My vision is blurry. My shoulders slump in defeat when I see the dark liquid flow across the floor as the remaining demons leave the house.

Mrs. Scott.

I turn slowly to see her on the floor.

I can't catch the air through my sobs, screams only echoing in my ears. I drop to the floor and tentatively stroke her hair from her face, but it does nothing because I'm not there.

I sit, useless. My magick's hum is now silent. My thoughts are empty.

After the longest time I stand mechanically. The sun is rising through the glass windows in the entry way. I feel as if it's been only a few minutes, but it's most likely been an hour or more. I have to do something. She can't stay like this. It's not right.

A reflective light catches my eye, and I see that Mrs. Scott is clutching something in her hand. It's the necklace Sabine gave me—my mother's necklace. I want to feel Mrs. Scott's warm hug but instead it's her voice that rings in my ear.

"Ah, my sweetheart, Willow. I don't have much in magick but have attached what I have to this to be with you. As above and so below, blessed be your path." Her voice is gone and her warmth fades.

I wipe my face of the tears that remain and reach for the necklace, the pentacle of the Goddess. It slips through my fingers. I can't hold it.

If I ever thought I would be able to escape the choice for the crown, it's resolved in this moment— my choice was made by the person in the cloak when they ordered Mrs. Scott's death. They and that devil who did it will regret it.

I need help, but I don't know what to do. If Rhydian found me in the woods, could he help me here? Trying to use my magick, I silently call to Rhydian in my head. I don't know how to get out of this in-between, this hell. Will I be stuck here forever?

His voice, a welcome retreat from my drowning thoughts: "Willow? Where are you?"

I try to explain in my mind, wondering if it will work and trying not to hold my breath. A moment later I'm shielding my eyes from a bright light at the open door. Rhydian walks through as my Guardian and savior. I run to him and hug him for dear life. He's here. I can touch him and he can touch me. I sob into his shoulder. He's found me in this black-and-white in-between.

"How did you . . . ? No one else can see or hear me. How did you? Thank you, thank you, thank you."

"I'm blooded to you; I will always find you." He pulls back from holding me and sees Mrs. Scott. "We need to go; they will find you in this split plane. The rift is helping to conceal you, but not for long."

I nod in agreement. "Rhydian, Wiccans were here with demons."

He continues to look at Mrs. Scott. I can't bear it. I know she's gone, but I can't see it anymore. If I do, I'll be torn apart. I need to keep it together.

A bright light appears and Dr. Evan is running at us, sliding to a stop.

"Dr. Evan?"

"Get away from him! He's a Guardian sent to kill you!" Dr. Evan yells. "Theon, now!"

A boy with long hair, Theon, appears from behind Dr. Evan and shifts into battle gear like a knight, similar to the Guardians but different. He draws a sword and advances so quickly that Rhydian pushes me to the side and morphs into his sleek armor. He is dark and brooding, his face not covered like Theon's.

Clank. The swords meet and they are fighting—but for what? Me?

Evan grabs my arm and transports us. My eyesight blurs as swords hit again and lights erupt. I say a silent prayer to anyone who will listen to protect Rhydian and to get me out of this nightmare.

CHAPTER 11

When I open my eyes I'm in the familiar surroundings of Dr. Evan's office. I push myself up on the chaise lounge.

"Don't you dare say it—" I start. My magick' s familiar hum is a buzz in the back of my head. He knew. He knew about the Guardians and what's going on and what I am. He knows.

"Say what, Willow? That was really close."

I start to think that everything that has happened in the last several days isn't real; it was all in my head.

I'm losing my mind.

What about Mrs. Scott's death? The demons and Wiccans in my home? Rhydian fighting that demon in the woods? The Guardians? Sabine and my father?

Magick?

I go to touch my necklace—my mother's necklace—but remember it's with Mrs. Scott, and I look at Dr. Evan to center myself. He's in different clothes from when I was here last. Isn't he?

"Willow. Focus, Willow," he says. His voice is smooth, calming.

The office is twisting and turning. It's like those fun-house mirrors at the fair. I am definitely losing it. I close my eyes and breathe deeply.

My stomach is in knots.

"What's up with her?" Theon asks, entering the room. Reality snaps back into focus. Small horns are revealed through his long, messy hair. He's part demon? Or something else entirely.

"Whoa, look at her hands." Theon is holding his helmet and puts it on the desk in the middle of the room. "By the way, the Guardian is fine. Good fighter. I think I may find him just for fun next time." Theon stretches out his shoulders and neck. "Nice to get a workout with someone of similar skills."

Evan rolls his eyes.

I peer down and see that the scrolling pattern on my hands and arms is pulsing and flowing like a river. I push my sleeve up and see the design flowing there, too, and then push it back in place. I feel a hum inside as it flows up my arms and down my shoulders. It's impressive and it comforts me, makes me feel brave.

I'm not okay with being in the presence of a demon and I don't trust Dr. Evan as a result of his being with Theon. Something is off here and I'm tired of not knowing. I grit my teeth to steady myself.

"Fancy that," Dr. Evan says, looking at my hands. He takes off his jacket and throws it on a chair in front of his desk. "Hell of a night. You know the Guardians have orders to kill you. What were you doing at your house with a Guardian? Have others come to your house?"

"So, it's fair to say you aren't a real doctor?" I spit the question at him.

He shakes his head to confirm.

"As you're condemning me for being around a Guardian, exactly who are you, and why should I trust you?" I point at him in my emboldened state. I trusted this man—my doctor—to put me under hypnosis. Evan stands in front of me but Theon stays at the desk working on a laptop. Probably a smart move.

"I really wanted more time for us to get to know one another before Sabine came riding in on her dark horse," Evan says.

"What does that mean? And how do you know Sabine? I assume you're a Wiccan?" I stand and pace the floor.

"Yes, I am Wiccan. Sabine's a bit complicated when it comes to me. I'm the bastard child of Harkin MacKinnon."

We're family? He doesn't seem to notice my utter surprise and my hinged mouth open.

He continues, "Harkin and I had an interesting relationship, to say the least, but Sabine and I . . . well, I was the reminder she hated and ignored."

"You're my uncle." I stand still, rooted. "Did you grow up with my . . . my mother?"

His face softens at the mention of my mother.

"I lived in the house with her from birth. I grew up with Liam and Nuala in the highlands of the

Ember region in Edayri. The MacKinnon manor. It wasn't an awful childhood, but I stayed in the shadows as the dirty little secret of the family. Liam and Nuala were the joy of Harkin and the noble Wiccan covens." He pauses and turns away from me. "Nuala was wonderful to me. I was her baby brother." He smiles, and it reminds me of a photo of my mother where she's holding me, laughing and her eyes sparkling. "When Liam left it hurt, but when Nuala ran away with Aiden, it broke the foundation of the family. Harkin became bitter and I became a bargaining chip to retain the royal line and royal coven positioning."

I walk over to Evan, wanting to comfort him. He's my uncle, but I'm cautious. Now that I'm looking, I see familiar features of my mother in him—dark blond hair and dark blue eyes.

"Why didn't you tell me this in the beginning? Why pose as my doctor?" I ask. "Do you get how messed up that is? Surely it's illegal."

"I hope you can forgive me for that," he says. "I needed to ease my way in. Nuala and I used to do it when we were younger—come together in magickal riffs and alternate thought planes it's a tease on reality but those in it can talk safely, or in my case, play when I was younger without outside influences. It was a safe way for me to reach you. I knew you were bound from your magick. You see, Sabine and everyone else thinks I'm dead."

I step back. Theon, who's been quiet till now, chuckles under his breath. "Surprise."

"And who are you?" I snap.

"I'm Theon. No familial relation." He goes back to typing.

"He's a good friend," Evan says. "Come on, let's get you something warm to drink and talk more." He walks to a door and I follow.

The familiar office gives way to an apartment. It's confusing. I've been to the medical suite before, but it wasn't someone's home. Through the door there's an open floor with a spacious, sparse modern living room and kitchen. I sit at the bar while Evan prepares tea.

"Just so you know, Rhydian has gone rogue from the Guardians. He wasn't there to hurt me, only to protect me. He said he's blood bonded or something like that. I dunno."

Evan raises his eyebrows.

"What?" I ask.

"Do you know what that means?" Evan says. "To have a blooded vow, a bond?"

I shrug. I figure it's like the Secret Service, but I don't want to sound foolish, so I kept my mouth shut.

"He made a bonded blood pact, and his life and duty are yours."

"Okay . . ."

"Without his choice in the matter. Or yours, I might add." He sounds bitter. "You took his vow lightly."

"I didn't, he did this with my father."

"He will die for you, literally. Should something happen to you, he will follow to protect you in

Heaven, Valhalla, or in the Elysian Fields—whichever you're inclined to believe."

I didn't know what to think or say. Why would someone commit to something like that without knowing the other person? I don't know a lot about Rhydian, considering I just met him, but I can't understand why he'd do this without knowing me at all. I don't want to be a puppet master in someone else's life.

"Yeah, a little crazy, huh? Let me tell you: Wiccans, in general, are stubborn in their profound beliefs, one of which is the dependence on royal blood lines from the Goddess. Lucky you for being in that line of fire."

"Sure, lucky me." I feel like I may collapse I'm so tired. I see the sun through the windows, bright and high in the sky. I have no idea of the time, but it feels like I've been up for over a day.

We finish our tea and Theon comes out of the office. Out of his armor, he resembles a grunge teenager about my age. "Evan, we need to get her to the High Coven. They're meeting tomorrow. Sabine called the meeting, as you anticipated."

Evan nods, but I disagree.

"I need to go home and talk to my father."

Evan nods his head up at Theon. He shakes his head no.

"Share with the class, please. What?" I demand.

Theon turns and goes back to the office.

"Just tell me."

"Your father is missing. I've been trying to reach

him. Theon is excellent at tracking and he hasn't had any luck, either."

I stand and pace. "What? Oh no. That's why Mrs. Scott—" Her name hangs on my tongue and chokes me. I wipe the immediate tear that falls. "She was looking for both of us."

"I'm sorry about Mrs. Scott. Really, I am. I think whatever form of magick she had, she imparted to you. It's why your magick is flowing; it's compounding. It takes a lot out of a person."

I don't like that he talks about Mrs. Scott in the past tense. I don't like that he knows she gave her magick to me. He may be my uncle, but something is off.

I brush the faded white designs on my hands and fingers. They come to life and glow blue. "Can one person give their magick to another?"

Evan sits down on a modern sofa that faces the windows.

"Only someone very powerful can loan magick, but this is dark magick. You can only impart magick in death or send it to the void."

I immediately think of Father. He has been teaching me about dark magick, which is his heritage. It isn't like most conventional magick, apparently.

"This place is well protected, so you can stay here as long as you'd like. However, in return, I need you to take me to the High Coven tomorrow," Evan says.

"How would I take you? I don't even know where it will be."

"It's not a problem. It's at the Hallowed Hall in

Edayri by the Lunar Fields, but the invite will have a magick seal that will only allow those invited. Those in attendance will be your High Coven when you take the crown." His eyes sparkle and the hair on my neck stands on end. I try to keep myself calm.

"What does that mean? My High Coven? Is that like a council or something?"

"Kind of, they hold power over commanding the Guardians, especially in the absence of the Crown." He traces a pentagram on his palm and says, "They represent royal rule over Edayri by the elements; air, fire, earth, and water."

"What's the last element at the top?" A yawn escapes my mouth. "Sorry about that. I haven't had any sleep for over twenty-four hours."

"It's the spirit element."

"So we need to go there to get the price off my head with the other Guardians?"

"Other Guardians?"

Another yawn escapes. "Yes, the rogue Guardians are helping me."

Evan nods and leads me to a guest room with a private bathroom. His apartment isn't large but it's certainly comfortable. I decide to take a shower. Unable to hold it in any longer, I melt into my emotions. My tears and anguish for Mrs. Scott, my fear of what's happening, and my hopelessness at being able to change any of it pour out of me. The water turns cold and I lean away from the tile and turn off the water. By the time I pull myself off the floor and get out, the mirror isn't foggy.

I brush my hair and examine the scrolling design that extends from my arms and shoulders down my back like a pair of wings. It's beautiful, but it disappears and is barely visible unless I call to my magick. When I call, it lights up in a neon blue, purplish color similar to the light ball I can conjure with my hand.

I put on the pair of shorts and T-shirt that Evan has laid on the bed. They fit me and it makes me uncomfortable. Was he anticipating my stay here? I pace the room and go to the window. Looking out, I see we are several floors up in a city I don't recognize. I hear Theon and Evan talking in the living room. I'm tired, but I want to listen to what they're saying. My magick flowing, I get into bed and concentrate on self-projection. I haven't tried this before—I'm not sure it will even work—but I'm pleasantly surprised when it goes smoothly. I ghost down the hall and hang back so I can hear but not be seen.

"Evan, I know you're doing this for Meghan. You should tell her what Sabine and Harkin did."

"In time. But first, we need to stay on task. It's tough to manage as it is. She's a lot like Nuala. She'll run; I feel it. We need to keep her away from that rogue group and especially Rhydian," Evan says. "She says he's bonded to her by blooded vow. Can you reach out and tell her we have Willow? Maybe she'll back off on her primary agenda."

"Fine. If I don't come back, it's because she's killed me," Theon says.

They both laugh and Evan claps Theon on the back. Evan goes to his office and Theon opens the balcony doors. I pull myself back to the bed and my eyes flutter closed.

Where is my father?

Exhaustion overtakes me to the unease of nothingness.

I toss and turn, feeling wetness around me. I open my eyes to darkness and cold. I push myself up from a concrete floor.

What—?

The liquid in front of me is dark and thick. I stand and my eyes start to adjust until I can make out bars ahead of me. I'm in some sort of jail cell? I step over the liquid and hear a shifting noise behind me. I turn but can't make anything out. I know I'm not alone.

"Hello?" I whisper.

The voice that answers croaks and is strained: "Willow? Sweetheart?"

My father! "Dad! Where are you?"

"Don't move. I don't know how long—the connection isn't strong. I'm very weak."

I call my magick and it flows, making the square cell glows. My father is lying on a cot in the corner. His face is beaten and bloody. He seems like he's lost weight; his clothes pool around him. I want to step forward, but I'm afraid about the connection he spoke of. If I lose it, I lose him.

"Willow . . . Evan. His agenda is beyond yours. Go to the High Coven and get their support with the Guardians. Find me and Lucy."

My heartbeat thunders in my chest at Lucy's name.

"Rhydian." He coughs, blood on his lips. "Rhydian, seek him out. Call to him, he'll come to you." He coughs again. The tears flow down my cheeks and I clench my fists at my side.

"I love you, Daddy. I'll find you and Lucy." My voice shakes.

"I love you too."

The creak of a door sounds. He waves his fingers and blurs before my eyes. All I can do is scream in anguish, and I wake up in the darkness of Evan's guest room. Heavy steps are coming. This real life nightmare is getting worse and I don't have time to curl up and dissolve into nothing.

Theon opens the door. "Are you—?"

My magick is fueled by fear and anger. I command the air around me and throw him back down the hall into the opposite wall. I envision my jeans and shoes and they materialize on my body.

I walk through the door to find Theon out cold.

The satisfaction of eliciting a physical outcome on someone—wow, what a rush. I should be scared of it, but I need to leave and I refuse to contemplate it now. I step over Theon and feel my magick hum. It feels like I can't transport from inside the apartment. I go to the balcony, but it's locked.

Determined and feeling powerful beyond what I've tried before, I step back, wave my hand, and command the glass to break in the sliding door. Evan comes running out of the office. I ignore him and step outside, quickly transporting myself to a white sandy beach from my childhood.

They're gone along with the apartment. The wind blows in my face and the moon lights up the beach. I came to this beach with my dad when I was little after mother had passed away, after the accident. My resolve is stone: I'll get my dad and Lucy back, and nothing and no one is going to get in my way. In fact, it excites me that someone might try. Power and strength radiate through me with the hum of my magick. Shouldn't I be scared? I'm not. I'm in control.

I take in the smell of the ocean and silently send a message: *Rhydian, find me.*

PART III

Fate whispers to the girl,
"You cannot withstand the storm."
The girl whispers back:
"I am the storm."

CHAPTER 12

I sit in the sand mindlessly touching my mother's necklace, watching the gentle waves lap the beach in a mesmerizing rhythm. It's distracting, quieting my mind. I don't hear or see Rhydian arrive, but suddenly he's sitting next to me.

"Hey."

"Hi."

He seems comfortable watching the waves with me in silence. I'm nervous to talk to him now that I know more about things—the crown, the political coups, the blood vow. For some reason, I want him to agree with all that I need to do. I know he won't let me down with the blood vow. I wonder if he has no choice but to agree if I give him an option. The thought hangs in the back of my mind—would he follow without the blood vow?

"I need you to go with me to the High Coven in a few hours," I say.

He raises his eyebrows at me. "Which is a dangerous mission. Why?"

The word dangerous excites me. What is with my magick? It's nudging me, taunting me to flex my power. I'm no longer nervous to do something wrong. I know my thoughts and will that drive it, but I'm still not familiar with Edayri and the realm in general. I need guides.

"I need the Guardians' help to rescue my father and my friend. They have been taken and are being tortured to lure me out."

He turns to me. "You have Guardians—me and the guys. You don't need the High Coven involved in this. They'll turn it into a political move to tie you down." He thrusts his hand into his hair. "Where did they take you? Evan and Theon. I've been looking for you. All of us, I mean—Tullen, Quinn, even Cross." He smirks on the last name.

"Even Cross, you say?" I peer sideways at him.

Rhydian snickers. "Cross is pretty much grumpy about everything, but he's loyal almost to a fault. He isn't too keen on the royal caste system, though, and blames Harkin for a battle that shouldn't have taken place. But his loyalty to his father and what the Guardians generally stand for keep him with us. He likes to challenge everything and everyone." He rolls his eyes, as if reliving something that recently happened with Cross.

"Oh, good. I thought it was just me."

Rhydian and I laugh together. I'm comfortable around him. He's handsome but not overly distracting like when we first met. Still, I find it hard not to stare at him. His perfect white smile and full lips draw me in.

"Seriously though, I was shocked to see Evan. I thought he was dead," Rhydian says. "What did he want? Where did he take you and how did you get away?"

Do I reveal everything that I've learned to Rhydian? Maybe he knows more than I do. There's just something about him that makes me trust him, besides knowing that he's made a blooded vow and that my father asked me to seek him out.

I stare down at my sand-covered feet and tell him everything.

He is taking it all in when I ask, "Why are you and the others rogue to help me? Out of duty? Because I don't want that. I don't want the responsibility of anyone getting hurt because of me. I didn't ask for any of this." I especially don't want to make someone do something they don't want, like this blood vow. Why would he do that?

"When we were in school for training to be Guardians, we took oaths to protect the crown and its interests. Now the crown is absent, and the High Coven is taking on that responsibility and warping it. You are the crown, whether or not you've completely accepted that yet." His eyes search mine. "There was an idea that the crown could be divided and bring harmony before the Convergence. Many are starting to recognize the Convergence is already beginning to happen. The truly powerful are afraid—afraid that you're an outsider and that your youth will bring change that doesn't suit them. I have the feeling, along with others, that you're the one who can bring about a positive change."

"Ah. So it's not all about me then?" I tag his shoulder gently and he chuckles.

His smile and relaxed demeanor are so attractive.

"What's the Convergence?" I ask.

His lips purse. "That is tough to answer."

"Why?"

He shrugs. "Because it's mythical and no one really understands it. There are some old histories that say the Convergence happens every two thousand years or so within the various realms to bring them together. Some say it's a contest of sorts; others say it's colonization and a war of territories." He runs his hand through his hair, revealing a golden ring clipped to the top of his ear. "The thing is, as a Guardian, I've been training for this unknown threat of the Convergence for a couple of years. If you ask Tullen, he'll say it's coming in the next year or so. If you ask Quinn, he'll say the Convergence is a myth. I don't know what I believe, but I do feel a change from others like the valkyrie and demons. They seem to be preparing themselves, and since Wiccans are not always on friendly terms with other species, no one shares information. It's tragic if you ask me."

I am so out of my depth here. As Queen, I will have to address this Convergence, and yet I'm only seventeen. A few weeks ago my biggest decision was which cell phone case I wanted to buy. I stressed about the start of school and who would be in my classes, wondering if Daniel and I would see much of each other because of our different schedules.

Daniel.

Have I already forgotten my life?

My father was right—magick will come whether I want it or not. But will my friends and Daniel accept me still? Am I still me? I'm just enhanced; surely I can go back to my life once I find Father. He and I can put something in place that allows me to finish out my senior year and got to college. I hope.

Rhydian and I sit in silence. I notice that our hands are close to each other in the sand as we sit back and watch the sun peeking over the horizon. The colors in the sky are amazing, purples that combine with blue hues and give way to red and orange.

"Nice spot you've chosen."

"Yes. Yes, it is. It was simpler when I was here before." I let the memory hang on my tongue and reminisce privately about my father holding my six-year-old hand. Rhydian reaches and gently brushes his fingers on mine.

I look back at Rhydian. "It's about time. We should probably go."

We arrive in Edayri at the Lunar Fields, and it's like my soul knows where I belong. There is lushness and life in the greenery all around, from the grass to the perfectly manicured trees to the gently rolling hills. The Hallowed Hall sits ahead of us with beautiful gardens and fountains. There are people scattered throughout the space, talking and sitting together. All are dressed in cloaks of various colors and patterns. I glance down at myself and conjure a red cloak similar to those in front of me by only thinking about it. Rhydian nods at the change in my clothes. My ability to use my magick is becoming easier, even if the chatter in my head hasn't stopped.

Rhydian turns to me. He's very close. Our agreement is that I will enter the Hallowed Hall by myself and he will wait on the outskirts while the others cause some chaos elsewhere in the Lunar Fields to distract the Guardians searching for me. The Guardians are ordered to retain me if they catch me. Where it goes from there is unclear, but I have the impression from Evan that someone in the High Coven is pulling strings to be rid of me.

"It's hard for me to leave you here," Rhydian breathes.

He's too close, and I could easily be pulled away from what I need to do, from who I am. I'm with Daniel, even if that seems like a lifetime ago. I step away from him.

"Thank you for the lift. I'll ring you when I'm done." I tap my head, grin, then walk down the path to the entry of the lush gardens.

My ability to walk into the Hallowed Halls unnoticed is abated with the arrival of Sabine. She stands out in her deep purple cloak. There are many eyes on her as she sees me.

"Willow?"

My magick stirs in my hand with nervous energy.

Is Sabine someone I can trust? Will she allow me to attend? Or is this over, right here and now?

I nod but keep my hood in place.

"I'm glad you're here. It's a good step to meet with your High Coven and show your intent and goodwill toward our ways," she says.

Is this a trap?

I follow Sabine through the tall wooden doors. Inside, Sabine walks through the open courtyard to another pair of similarly arched doors. She places her hand on the door and it glows before opening. I follow her inside.

The room has a circular table at its center around which sit four purple-cloaked figures, all female. Their eyes watch me as I follow Sabine to the empty seat. The woman who ordered Mrs. Scott's death wore a purple cloak. I shake my head trying to stay focused, for my father.

"And who is this?" one asks with a snicker.

Another claps her hands together and rubs them vigorously, as if excited for some major event.

Sabine stands by her chair. "You would have felt someone who didn't belong enter this room. May I introduce Willow, my granddaughter and successor to the crown." She sounds proud.

She introduces the snickering woman as Celestia and the excited one as Pansy.

I gently pull my hood back to reveal myself fully to the High Coven. They are assessing me just as I am assessing them.

Then the flurry of questions begins.

Celestia is first. "So, your intention is to come into your birthright?"

"How can you do that when you're an outsider?" the one with white hair asks.

"Have you used your magick yet?" Pansy is all smiles.

Celestia sneers. "What is your elemental magick? I bet she isn't even aware!"

Only three of the women at the table participate in the questions and discussion. The one to my right is surveying her fingernails, looking bored. She seems rather young among these women, not much older than me.

Part of me wants to run out the door. The other part of me wants to scream. I always hated having to do presentations in class and this feels no different, except that I'm less prepared on a topic I can't research.

"Stop throwing questions at her," Sabine thunders over the chatter.

I take advantage of the silence. "I've come here to ask for your approval and assistance. I need the Guardians; my father and friend have been taken."

Sabine's hand flies to her chest. "By who?"

"I imagine the same demons and Wiccans who came to my home and murdered a member of my family, Mrs. Juliette Scott."

The one who was staring at her nails is now watching me intently. Sabine introduces her as Aren.

"I understand that this High Coven has control over the Guardians," I say, "and I would like to—"

"No, no, no," Pansy says, bouncing her leg.

Sabine lays her hand on her shoulder. "Let's hear her out. Would you deny her only—"

"Sabine, we are set for you to take the crown," the white-haired one, introduced as Renata, says through tight, thin lips.

Sabine shakes her head, face flushed. So, Sabine can step in for the crown? Why didn't she say anything when we first met? I wonder why she wouldn't take the crown; it would be logical. She's from here and is far more powerful than me.

There's a shift in the room. Renata's statement is echoed by Celestia, Pansy, and Aren.

This is a lost cause. They don't want me here; they have plans to move forward without me. My magick stirs against the hypocrisy of this High Coven that claims to serve the crown—my crown.

Idiots. I don't need them. I walk back toward the door I had come through. "Thank you for your time."

"You can't accept the crown without our support," says Celestia, in a lower voice that makes the hair on my neck rise.

Are you going to stop me? I wonder to myself. That could be quite fun. Instead, staring directly into Celestia's cold, dark eyes, I say, "Actually, I only need the Goddess. Get ready to be replaced. I believe the crown decides who is in the High Coven along with all other things in Edayri. You should be ready for some changes, ladies."

Empowered by my father and from what I've read in the Book of Shadows, I slam the door behind me.

A nervous breath escapes my throat and my hands shake slightly. I leave my hood down and walk through the open hall, out the front of the building, and through the gardens. Several seem to recognize me. I sense Rhydian and the others on the outskirts of the gardens.

Sorry, boys. Plans have changed!

I continue to stare straight ahead and go directly to the fountain at the center of the gardens. When I turn, Sabine and the other members of the High Coven are at the steps of the building. Guardians in armor come toward me from both sides of the building.

Do they want to detain me? They want to test what I can do and who I am? Fine! I don't need them. Rhydian is right.

My magick is eager and so am I. Without thinking much about it, I thrust my hands above my head and lightning shoots upward into the clear blue sky. I control the environment here; the clear day becomes my storm of warning. The wind picks up and the clouds move in on my command. The designs on my hands and arms glow with pulsing bright light. The people around the fountain have moved away, but not far. They seem torn between fascination and self-preservation.

All attention is on me and I relish it. I sneer at the High Coven. "Does this satisfy you?" I shout.

The people retreat further away and the Guardians become cautious in their advance. I command the wind around me and rise above the ground, peering down at them—the High Coven, Guardians, and other Wiccans—searching to see if one will challenge me. No one does. The High Coven is in shock as their cloaks whip in the wind I have conjured, mouths gaping.

Sabine's eyes are wide, her red hair flying behind her as she braces against the wind.

Rhydian, Tullen, Quinn, and Cross transport to me and take positions around me like a compass. The Guardians stop advancing.

I float down to the center of my rogue Guardians and protectors. Cross and Rhydian step aside as I walk forward to face the High Coven.

I project my voice. "I do accept my duty, the crown, and my birthright. These are my royal guard —" I gesture toward Rhydian, Tullen, Cross, and Quinn. "They are not rogue from their duties as Guardians, but serve in a new capacity as a personal guard for the Queen."

My choice is proclaimed as my father advised. Then the tide turns and all who are present lower to one knee, bowing their heads—including the High Coven on the steps of the Hallowed Halls.

"Now, someone tell me where my father is!"

When you have power, it's interesting to see how others back off when you show it, but not before. It could be so easily abused, and part of me wants to abuse it. Why don't I? Because that's not who I am. Or who I was? This new part of me is addictive. My magick is so powerful that my whims can be realities. It's a little scary.

My center—my base—is my home, and after knocking the Wiccan High Coven off their pedestal with my display of magick, I transport myself back there. They didn't know anything about my father. It felt like a waste of time.

I feel like a visitor at the front door. I hesitate to open it, knowing that the chaos from the other night will still be present. Mrs. Scott needs to be put to rest and I'm not sure how to do that, but she deserves better than to lie in the foyer. I've aged five years from the girl who met her grandmother only a few days ago. My sense of time is warped; has it really only been a few days?

I take a deep breath and open the door. I'm caught by surprise: nothing is messed up or wrecked. The floors are clean, the furniture upright, the lights back on walls and hanging from the ceiling. The large, round table is in the middle of the foyer with a bouquet of flowers. Someone has to be here. I pray it is my father, knowing full well that isn't likely. No one seems to know anything about the whereabout of him or Lucy. Maybe it was all a dream and Mrs. Scott is fine?

"Hello? Anyone here?" I raise my voice, hoping she will answer me.

There's no response and, although I expected none, my heart sinks. Someone must have cleaned the house, but who? Where is Mrs. Scott?

The back door opens and I walk toward the kitchen. It won't be Mrs. Scott, but I can't help it—I want it to be her so badly. When I see Rhydian, Cross, and Tullen enter, I try to lift my mood, but I can't put up the facade anymore. Tears stream down my face.

Tullen hugs me. "Willow, I'm sorry for everything that has happened, and all that will." I don't know what to say to that, but he saves me the trouble. "It's part of your journey. It's a tough one, but I certainly think you have the guts to face it." He goes to the fridge and grabs a water.

Cross chuckles. "That show ya put on at the Hallowed Hall certainly has got folks talkin'. All the groups are a little intimidated by yer show of power. Whoever thought the monarchy was dead didn't realize it had just changed zip codes. What's ya next move?"

I squint at him sideways.

"What? Come on, Willow, I'm not always of the opposite opinion." His smirk tells me otherwise.

Tullen throws Cross a bottle of water and they sit at the kitchen table, each grabbing an apple from the bowl in the center.

Rhydian is studying me, his hazel eyes searching. Then it hits me: they are the ones who cleaned everything up. Mrs. Scott's body must be somewhere safe. His nod at my questioning look is all I need. I hug him. "Thank you. I—" My voice chokes with emotion.

I walk to Tullen and Cross at the table and smile despite my waterworks. Cross looks away as if he doesn't want to reveal his own emotions. For a big brute, he does have a sensitive side. I think I like him more than when I first met him.

Tullen excuses himself and transports back to the Hallowed Hall, where Quinn is discussing issues with Eoin, Head of the Guardians. My display brought concerns to the surface regarding the High Coven's abuse of power since Harkin's passing.

The quiet moment of sitting ends when Rhydian looks out the bay window from the kitchen. "Willow, you have visitors. One of them is that valkyrie friend of yours."

The doorbell rings thirty seconds later. When I answer it, Emily grabs me into a hug and whispers in my ear, "I'm so happy you're okay. I told them every-thing so we can rescue Lucy and your dad."

"How do you know?" I ask.

"I fought them; they wanted me but took Lucy. They already had your dad." Emily wrings her hands, walking into the house.

Daniel has his hands in his pockets and is tenta-tive about coming in. Marco gives me a quick hug, then takes a step back when Rhydian and Cross enter the foyer.

"So, let's all get to know one another. Follow me to the living room," Emily says with a smile. Emily ushers everyone except Daniel and me.

Shutting the front door behind him, Daniel takes a step toward me and hugs me tight, just holding me. I melt into the familiar comfort, the normalcy of just us that I miss. For a moment I can almost forget the nightmare.

"Wills, I've been so worried about you." He leans back to stares in my eyes, reaching a part of my heart that squeezes at his declaration. "I'm so sorry about Mrs. Scott. Emily told us. It all sounds crazy. Are you okay?"

I have a hundred things I want to say, like, No, I'm not okay, and, I could be going crazy because it's not a dream. But instead, I say, "Yes, I'm okay."

He kisses me on my forehead and hugs me tight, then releases me. As we walk toward the formal living room, he hooks his arm around my shoulders. It feels normal and comfortable, like we're at school walking down the hall. Emily's voice comes loud from around the corner.

"Did you know Marco is a shapeshifter? My boy's a shifter and my girl's a Wiccan Queen."

The word "queen" makes me shudder. I don't know how I feel about it as a descriptor of who I am, but I guess I'd better get used to it.

I focus on the news about Marco, not doubting anything anymore. I'm surrounded by magick and different beings, from Guardians to valkyrie and now shapeshifters. At this point, I may be immune to knowing who is different; the shock of magick is becoming normal.

Rhydian tenses when Daniel and I walk into the room. I spy Emily deep discussion with Cross and Marco.

Rhydian walks over and shakes Daniel's hand, introducing himself and Cross.

"We may have a plan," Emily announces. She explains that Lucy and my father must be held somewhere in the Ember region. She's aware of a scry we can use to point us in the right direction if we bring familiar objects of my father's and Lucy's. It sounds like a long shot, but it's still the best idea we have.

"Tis well and good, but ya not leading this effort, we will." Cross gestures to Rhydian and himself. "Besides, we don't know ya."

Emily strides up to him, looking him over as he does the same. "And I don't know you. But that girl, is my dearest friend, my ride or die, so if you're going to lead an effort to help bring back her father and our best friend you better have a damn good plan."

"What about a bait and switch plan instead?" Rhydian asks.

Cross nods in agreement.

Emily eyes Rhydian. "Like what?"

"Me," I say before Rhydian and Cross can answer. "Whoever plans to overtake the crown really wants me—my magick, that is. It might be Evan; I overheard him talking."

Emily shakes her head quickly. "No, Evan wouldn't hurt you, Will." She pauses and looks at Rhydian. "Did you tell her what they did to him and Meghan?"

"Who is Meghan? And how do you know Evan, my uncle? Do you know Theon?"

Before she can answer, Rhydian does. "His wife, Meghan." He paces in front of Cross and continues. "Harkin arranged a marriage for Evan to a Noble Coven Wiccan, but Evan didn't want to have anything to do with it. He was an outcast because he was a bastard. His bloodline was in question, including where his power came from.

"It wasn't long after your mother passed away that Evan ran away with Meghan, who is of fae and demon descent. They married in secret. When they were found by the Guardians and put in front of the High Coven, Harkin was embarrassed and angry. He felt betrayed by Evan and tried to take his blooded heritage from him, which in turn would remove any familial physical Wiccan powers that descended from him to Evan, and condemned him to live outside of

Edayri. This caused Evan's demon side to become evident. Harkin's infidelity became clear to the world, and out of anger and embarrassment at his exposed secret, he . . . he executed Meghan.

"Because Evan is not full Wiccan but also part demon, the effort to remove his magick blood only empowered him. He's been rallying with demons and fae to take down the royal caste system entirely."

Why didn't my father tell me any of this? I can't imagine the hurt Evan carries. Daniel hugs me closer to him in comfort.

"They killed her? Why didn't the High Coven, or Sabine for that matter, do the same with my father or me?" I feel sick to my stomach.

"Your father's family is high in the noble caste system; they were part of the High Coven at one time. You're pure Wiccan and your mother was next in line for the throne. Sabine, really can't take the crown for her own, but I'm sure she would want the family royal legacy to remain. It's certainly not an even playing field for Evan. Everyone thought he was dead, so it's not clear to me," Rhydian replies.

"What is Theon? He's always with Evan," I ask Emily.

"I believe one of Evan's cousins on his mother's side. Theon is also part Wiccan and demon, like Evan."

How does she know this, and why would she not have said anything before? Then I remember that the last time I saw Emily, Rhydian was saving me from a blood warrior demon. I move away from everyone and walk toward the window. Silence haunts me for the death Evan has endured. We have too much in common now, when I think about Mrs. Scott.

When I turn around, Cross is leaning on the living room entryway post. "I say our best hope is to dangle Willow to capture Evan and Theon. They must have your father and your friend. They're the only ones who would get a payoff for yer cooperation."

Rhydian agrees, but Daniel objects. "You can't use her as bait. You don't know who or what will come to her, so how can you control the scene?"

"You don't know what you're talking about. Willow is quite capable," Rhydian snaps.

I get between them and put my hand on Daniel's chest before he goes any further with Rhydian. "I'm all right," I say to Daniel. "It's a good plan and we have limited options." Daniel has no idea how I can handle myself now, or about the magick that is part of me.

"Okay," he says, "then I want to be there."

Rhydian laughs mockingly. "You are a casualty waiting to happen. You don't belong in Edayri."

Daniel gets up close to Rhydian. "You don't belong here. Wherever Willow goes, I'm going. Got it?"

"Your funeral," Rhydian says, closing what little gap they had.

Marco and I separate the two of them and I walk Rhydian across the hallway to the formal dining room.

"What are you doing? Daniel is my boyfriend," I hiss.

"He's going to get you hurt or killed. He's got no

skills and he's all territorial about what you can and can't do. Why would you put up with that?" Rhydian's voice keeps rising as he speaks. "Your world here is ending and you can't take him with you."

"You can't make that choice for me!"

"Which choice is that? Abandon your duties and play house with him? I can sense your thoughts and feelings for him." He sneers at Daniel as he speaks. Daniel sneers back.

I tug Rhydian's arm and move us so the others can't see. "What do you care, Rhydian?" I lower my voice.

He closes his eyes. "I don't. I'm sorry; it isn't my place to advise you on such matters." He turns to walk away, but I stop him.

"You're not saying something. Tell me."

I search his face, a face that only a few minutes ago that was so full of compassion but is now turned to stone. He looks down at me, his hazel eyes no longer depth of colors I can get lost in but cold and distant. His strong jaw is set, muscle ticking at the strain. He steps back from me, exhales, and messes his hair with one quick stroke of his hand. His full bottom lip is out as if he's pouting. I'm not sure what I want to hear, but something is off. I'm hurting him, but I'm not sure how it is possible when I've known him only for a few days.

He turns away from me and, as he walks out the entryway, says over his shoulder, "It's not important. You need to focus on other things."

I stand in the dining room alone.

CHAPTER 14

Bang. *Bang.*

"Open up! Police."

I walk into the foyer. Everyone seems preoccupied except for Daniel, who goes to the door.

It all happens in slow motion.

Daniel reaches for the door and is blown back with a giant ball of light, flying past me to the foot of the staircase. His head smacks down and blood spits out his mouth.

Cross, the closest to me, leaps and pushes me back into the dining room. Marco shifts into a tiger and charges the door. Raised voices are quickly drowned by a roar and growls from Marco. Rhydian is in full warrior mode, sword raised on three large demons who are entering the house.

Emily turns toward Daniel, then back around in brass armor with filigree gold designs. Her body is covered in key areas and open in others. Her helmet is the most ornate I've ever seen, like a war eagle with raised metal feathers back and down her head and a face structure that covers her forehead down to her nose.

She screams and throws her hands in the air, bringing them down with such force that the house shakes and lightning cracks outside. Cross rolls to the side of me and morphs into full warrior mode himself. His eyes are wide, watching her, and his crooked grin shows a dimple in his cheek.

Time catches up to my brain and everything speeds up.

Cross helps me up. "Ready? Let's get these fuckers."

I don't hesitate. This is my house! My hands are glowing and swirling with the design of my power. I follow him outside. Everyone is fighting all around the house, the double doors off their hinges.

Cross charges and I'm about to follow when I hear Daniel gurgle, struggling to breathe.

Daniel!

I am next to him in a split second. His body is lying oddly on the stairs and I'm afraid to move him. I kneel down and brush his hair from his eyes. "Daniel, can you hear me?"

His eyes move and he stares at me with utter pain. In all my power, I'm stunned. I can defend myself, but I have no idea what to do to help Daniel. I'm shaking as I listen to the fighting outside.

"Help me!" I scream at the open door. Daniel starts choking. "Rhydian, help me!"

Rhydian and Emily are at my side. Emily is

covered in blood. "As a valkyrie I might be able to bring him back as a warrior," she says. "You wouldn't have to be separated, but he won't be the same. Your choice." I look from Daniel to Emily to Rhydian. Cross and Marco are still fighting the demons on the front lawn.

My mouth dry, I swallow in brief contemplation of Em's offer. "No, no, no. I can't make that choice."

He's dying in front of me. "Rhydian, please heal him. Do everything you can. I don't have a clue what to do. Please! Oh my god, this can't be happening."

My hands glow and I try to touch him, but it burns me. Emily grabs me and pulls me away.

"This can't be happening!" I scream.

Rhydian calmly lays his hands on Daniel. His body lifts off the stairs and hovers as Rhydian guides him to the floor. His brows furrow and I feel his concentration. I am jealous that he knows exactly what to do, but I'm also so thankful for it.

I hear the fighting stop and time slows for me. Marco lies at my feet in tiger form while Cross stands next to us.

"It's going to take him if he's not careful. We need Quinn," Cross says under his breath.

"Can you go—"

Daniel gasps and bows his chest unnaturally. Rhydian leans further over him, like he's about to collapse with his shaking and straining hands hovering over Daniel. I break free from Emily and slide across the floor to the two of them.

Rhydian's face is strained, deep wrinkles on his

forehead. What have I asked for? What did I force Rhydian to do? Am I losing Rhydian? I will myself to loan part of my magick to him, laying my hand on his and removing it from Daniel's body. When I do, Rhydian collapses. Cross is there in a flash to catch him.

"This house is not safe. We need to leave," Cross says.

"We can't. Not while they're in this condition. I can hold the house," Emily says. She produces a staff out of thin air and hits the floor with it. A blanket of sheer light radiates from the staff along the floors, coating the walls, stairs, and spreading out from the front door over the entire house and grounds.

"Damn, that's hot," Cross says.

Emily winks at Cross.

Marco starts to roll on the floor. One minute he's covered in fur and the next his naked cappuccino skin is showing, back in his human form. I turn away to give him privacy and follow Cross to the formal living room, where he lays Rhydian on the sofa.

"Will Rhydian be all right . . . and Daniel?" I hesitate to add Daniel to my question. Rhydian was right when we argued earlier, but I had hoped I had more time with Daniel.

"Yeah, he'll be okay. Just needs to recharge. I think yer man needed it, though. Musta' been on the cusp. Rhydian's not a halfway guy. Guessing he wanted to make sure all the healing was right, but it puts him at risk. Glad you intervened. What did ya do?"

"I tried to give him part of my magick to use."

"Tis not possible."

"From my dark magick." I respond.

Cross's breath hitches in his throat. "Watch over him. I need to check on Daniel." Cross lifts his chin to me and I see Tullen transport in, battle-ready. He goes to Cross and Rhydian.

Marco stands next to Daniel, who lies on the dining room table. His chest rises and falls with each breath. He's going to be all right.

Rhydian is right: I can't be with him. He's in this situation because of me. My father's voice in my mind, repeats the words; inevitable—no choice.

I go to join the rest. I touch Daniel's hand and look at Marco. "I'm sorry. I would never put Daniel in danger." My voice cracks at his name.

"I understand that, Willow. I'm here for him though, not you." He says it matter-of-factly, but there is something hidden in his eyes. Gah. I hate me too right now.

I leave the dining room and come to stand in the foyer. Emily is there with her staff, protecting the house and everyone in it.

"Do you blame me for Lucy?" I ask her.

"No. Why would you ask that?" Her eyebrows draw together and her lips quirk to the side.

"I do." I sit on the stairs avoiding bloodstains, the living room on my right and the dining room on my left. I'm right in the middle, between Daniel and Rhydian. My familiar life and my new life.

CHAPTER 15

L ike a siren's call, a sharp noise bellows through the house. I yell and cover my ears, but everyone else just seems puzzled. I stand with my hands over my ears, yelling, "Can't you hear it?"

They all shake their heads no.

I follow the noise, rounding the back of the stairs to my father's office. The secret door is cracked open and a glow beckons me in. The sound pulses are lower and lower as I near. I'm nervous to walk into the hidden room, both afraid and hopeful about what I'll discover. Is it possible that my father and Lucy are there? I go into the chamber like a hopeful child but am disappointed when I see no one. The passageway door shuts behind me, enclosing me in the empty room.

The family Book of Shadows is not on the bookshelf where I placed it last; instead, it's open on the coffee table. An eerie, soft, white light glows from the pages, and the noise is gone.

The book summoned me.

I head to the overstuffed chair and touch the book. I snap my fingers back from the pages, feeling an electrical charge. The book comes to life and pages flip of their own accord. It stops on a blank page. I move the book closer to me and ink begins to appear.

It shows me what I desperately want to figure out: how to locate my father and Lucy.

The ability to find blooded family resides in a potion for transporting. The book lists out ingredients I'm not familiar with, but the most important is something from the blooded family member you're looking to find—including shared blood.

In my excitement, I pick up the book and walk from the hidden room, ready to show everyone our golden ticket. I stumble when I find everyone already in the office, including now-conscious Rhydian and Daniel.

They sit in opposite chairs, and I stop myself from heading directly to Daniel.

"Oh, thank god, you're okay! Both of you," I say.

Daniel adjusts himself slowly in the chair. "Thanks to Rhydian and you."

Rhydian nods to me. "Is that your family Book of Shadows?"

"Yes. How did you all realize I was in there?"

Marco pipes up. "I watched you go in and Tullen suggested it might be a Wiccan solitary circle space, so we stayed out here to wait on you. Plus, with Rhydian awake, he'd sense if you were in trouble."

I look at Rhydian, but he's avoiding my eyes.

Daniel cocks his head sideways at Rhydian.

"Thanks. I found a way of locating my father with a transporting potion. I think that if we locate him, Lucy should be nearby and we can rescue them both."

Emily looks at the book. "Great, but it's a blank page, Will."

"No, it was, but not anymore—can't you see?" It dawns on me then: they're not my family, of course they can't read it. "Don't worry, it's there—I'll read it aloud and we can work on it."

Cross shifts his legs and says, "Yes, and make enough so that several of us can go cause there's no way he's not heavily guarded what with his powerful magick. Whoever has yer father is most likely counting on ya to show up hot-headed and ready to do something stupid, and then they'll have ya both."

I smirk at Cross. "Hot-headed? I thought that was your title."

"Only when required." His dimple appears, and I swear Emily grins.

Tullen writes down what I read and then he, Cross, and Rhydian start gathering items from the hidden room. I go upstairs and pull a piece of my father's hair from his hairbrush. Upstairs, Duke is whining.

"Oh my god, Duke!" I open a closet door and my dog bounds out, jumps on me, and begins licking my face. I hug him, thankful he's okay in all this chaos. He follows me down the stairs and begins to growl deep in his throat. The hair on his back is ruffled. He's staring at Marco.

"Easy, Duke," Marco laughs. "I'm guessing he doesn't like cats?"

I laugh. "Easy, Duke."

Duke follows me into the room and lets Emily pet him, but he huffs and growls at Marco. When Cross and Rhydian walk in, Duke bounds over to them with his tail in full wag mode.

"Funny, a witch who likes dogs over cats. I think I like this about you," Rhydian says. Duke has made a new best friend, deserting me.

"We're ready. Quinn is on the way," Tullen says.

Daniel sits near the empty fireplace alone, looking out of place. Emily nods her head toward him and murmurs, "He can't go. It's too dangerous. Marco's going to take him home. Once I know where we're transporting, I'll come back for Marco if we need him."

I nod. I don't want to put anyone else in danger. I'm overwhelmed that Emily and Marco want to help me not just for Lucy but for my father too. Daniel would be in the middle of it as well, but he's not like us. Rhydian's right, it's inevitable there is no choice. My mind is set and it squeezes my heart.

The sun is starting to set and time seems to be getting away from us. Marco helps Daniel stand and I walk with them to the front door, past Emily's glowing staff that protects the house.

"Daniel, I'm really sorry you were—"

His finger is on my lips and he moves closer to me. "Let's not, okay?" He knows, that I would keep him safe in the only way I can. He won't let me say it.

He almost died. My friends are being used against me, and he doesn't belong in this craziness. Plus, it's all my fault that he's here at all. All I can do is nod.

"Be safe, Willow, and when you're back, let's talk. Good luck." Daniel wipes a stray tear from my face and kisses me, gentle and soft.

I don't want him to go with so much left unsaid. But it's not safe for him to be associated with me and I know this. I conjure my magick and command it to change his memory of the camping trip so that he thinks we were together all night, that I never left. When he wakes in the morning, an amicable and simple breakup. Our relationship ran its course. He'll be a happy Daniel with no regrets. I kiss him goodbye and he holds me to him. The memory I have conjured is released from me to him as I pull away.

"I love you."

"I love you, too." He releases me and is gone.

I should have taken note of that more. I touch my lips to feel his warmth leave me. I turn back to the house just in time to see Rhydian walking away.

"Rhydian, wait!"

He turns in the hallway to face me, rubbing the back of his neck and staring.

"Rhydian, Daniel's my . . . why are you . . . are you mad?"

"This is dangerous, is all. I'm not mad, but I don't need to be an audience member for your private moments." He nods to the front door.

"I don't understand why you're acting this way."

"There isn't anything to tell you that I haven't

already said." He huffs as if he's been holding his breath. "We have about an hour or so. Go get some rest. You're barely standing as it is."

Instead of following him into the office where everyone is gathered, I turn toward the stairs, where Emily is watching and holding her staff.

"I noticed what you did, Will."

I stop and hold the rail. It steadies me so I don't break into tears. "I had to, Em. He . . . I can't have him hurt because of any of this."

"I know," she says simply.

I walk upstairs to my room. I shower and change clothes, then lay on my bed with my eyes closed. I sink into my mattress, allowing the peacefulness of the dark to claim my mind quickly.

CHAPTER 16

The elevator is familiar, blankets tacked to its inside walls due to construction activities. I'm alone when I enter and hit the button for the sixth floor. Arriving, I turn to the right as I've done millions of times in the past and walk through the glass doors into an office.

The familiar blonde receptionist smiles and says that Dr. Bauche will be with me shortly. I pick up the two-month-old *People* magazine and flip through the pages. I've already read this magazine several times, but I keep flipping the pages to keep myself occupied. As I set the magazine down, Dr. Bauche appears in the hallway and calls my name.

Familiar and friendly as always, her hair is perfectly styled and she wears a dark pencil skirt, silk shirt, and black high heels. I follow her back to her office like I've done for so many sessions in the past.

"Willow, I'm actually surprised to see you. What brings you in today?" Her voice is soothing.

"A lot of changes in both my family and personal life," I say.

I tell her about everything, and I mean *everything*. Her response to the information is accepting. I tell her all the lies about where I come from, about meeting my long-lost grandmother and uncle, about discovering that I come from Wiccan royalty and I'm next in line for the throne. I tell her about the lure of the magick within myself, but how I also want what was my normal life. About Mrs. Scott and the threats on my life. I even tell her that a few of my friends are from the Edayri realm, and about the rogue, now royal, Guardians and how I don't want to disappoint them; I want to be a positive change in Edayri. I tell her how Daniel got hurt and almost died. I tell her about Rhydian's connection to me and his blooded vow. About how I am indebted to him, and the fact that I'm attracted to him even while I love Daniel. About how I let Daniel go to keep him safe. About how fatally broken my heart is at the loss of Mrs. Scott and Daniel.

I needed to release. I exhale heavy, yet my chest feels lighter.

"I'm sorry for the heartbreak, but that's a part of life that allows us to grow in companionship and in ourselves," she says. "Not what you wanted to hear?"

I shake my head and stare at my hands.

"How do I manage this? I'm going to burst. I'm scared this is all for nothing and that I'll fail at something, and I'm worried about who that will affect.

This crown, the anticipation of it, is overwhelming on top of my own selfish desires to stay the normal teenager I am."

"Those who accept and manage personal change well are those who are clear about what they want. They are also good at taking the necessary steps toward change and taking control of those elements that they can." She stands and circles to the front of her desk to sit on the corner. "Willow, I get the impression that you have decided how you feel about a few of the situations you've described to me. About the others, it's okay to take some time. Nothing is permanent."

She's right. I've been trying to speed my way through everything because I really haven't had a moment to pause. I've been running a marathon ever since Sabine came to dinner, since I walked into the Salem Woods.

"I want you to try some relaxation breathing techniques. They will help you to slow down as you face some of these challenges, when you note anxiety coming on. They help to center yourself and your thoughts, to clear out the noise so that you can focus on directive intention.

"Inhale and draw your breath in from your core. Pause and hold, but not uncomfortably, then release in a slow and steady stream of air. Count to yourself as you do both. Ten, twelve, fifteen seconds is typically good, though you can do longer if you have the time."

Dr. Bauche leads me in a routine to breathe in

deeply and exhale deeply, first for twelve seconds, then increasing the time with my next breaths. It really does help, and I'm better and more focused on the immediate tasks I need to deal with.

"Look at compartmentalizing issues, especially when faced with compounding issues and tasks. This will allow you to judge what to spend time on now versus later. It's a way to manage your time. The key is not to push off an issue and never address it. When you do that, it comes back to haunt you." She pats me on the hand and tells me time is up.

I follow her to the door. I don't really want to leave, but I know I should.

"Thank you for seeing me on such short notice," I say. "It was helpful . . . your guidance."

"Anytime, Willow. I'm here anytime you need me."

Her eyes are like mine, dark blue. Her chin and pert nose are just like mine. She opens the door and the office hallway morphs into my bedroom.

Awake, I rub my eyes and feel the wetness of my tears. Evan had said this is how he and my mother would communicate sometimes. Having access to my mother brings me comfort. Whether this is in my head or real doesn't matter. It doesn't even matter if she's really Dr. Bauche or Mom. I picture her as both, and maybe she is both. I cup my face and smile through my tears. Before I know it, I'm laughing and crying together. I have my mom with me and the idea of it is joyous.

A bump on my door tells me that Duke needs something and is on the other side waiting. I open the door and pet him on the head, then follow him down the back stairs to the kitchen. I put food in his bowl before I find Cross, Emily, Tullen, and Rhydian at the table, just waiting in silence. All eyes turn to me.

"Ready?" I ask.

PART IV

The girl throws her fist to the sky
"My destiny is my own!",
Fate is satisfied, for now . . .

CHAPTER 17

The potion that we've made is finished and ready. Quinn and Tullen are moving the foyer table into the formal living room. I have chalk in my hand, ready to draw the pentagram required to transport us wherever my father is being held.

"Start here in the north, where the stairs are." Rhydian points.

I nod and draw the pentagram star, then complete the circle. It feels strange to draw it, yet somehow familiar. I'm not much of an artist, but I think I do a decent job considering I have them all watching my every move.

"Okay, just so we all understand how this is going down," Cross says, "the plan is that Rhydian, Emily, and Willow will transport first. They'll scope out the area and, if able, Rhydian and Emily will return to us. If they can't both come, just Emily will return so that Rhydian can help protect Willow." Cross looks at Tullen and Quinn, who nod their heads in agreement.

Emily rolls her eyes. "Whatever. You know I'm the best regarding protection, and you've seen what she can do on her own. Your little hang-up that Willow needs *your* protection is cute though."

I love the confidence she has in me. I can't help but smile. The fact is, my magick is stronger now and I'm in control. Not everyone has real magick like mine in the Wiccan community. Plus, I think I scared the shit out of most of them at the Hallowed Hall. If whoever took my father and my best friend didn't see that display, hopefully they've heard about it by now.

"Let's go."

Rhydian is all business, pure focus. I envy him. I'm a mix of nerves, fear, and anger. Rhydian pours the potion into the bowl in the center of the pentagram. He, Emily, and I stand in the center of the circle. He nods to me, and I prick my finger and squeeze a drop of blood into the potion, add the last ingredient—my father's hair—then quickly grasp Rhydian and Emily's hands. Transportation is becoming easier for me, but this time the pull in various directions makes my stomach drop. The force of wind pushes us and I get thrown backward. My hand slips from Emily's and, in an instant, we fall into darkness onto a hard dirt floor.

I land on Emily and Rhydian touches my ankle. We all made it.

"Where the hell are we?" Emily whispers. "I can barely see anything."

"In some type of dungeon," Rhydian answers. He's already suited up in his sleek armor.

"Can you give us some of that glow magick, Wills?" Emily asks.

I light up my hand in a dull blue glow and the designs on my arm appear, the glow of magick flowing through them.

We're in some type of cell but the door is open. It is moist and damp, the air is stale with rust and mold. Outside the cell is a tunnel of aged stone and dirt floors. Lanterns spaced along the walls give some light to the left, but on the right the spacing is further apart, leaving everything dark.

"Which way do we go?" I ask.

"We need to split up," Rhydian replies.

I don't like that idea, but our options are limited. We take a step out of the cell and the barred door slams shut. The tunnel lights up entirely and an alarm sounds.

"Shit!" yells Rhydian.

"Bring it!" yells Emily.

I have a feeling we need to go left. I start running. "Come on, guys. This way!"

When I round the corner, I skid to a stop, less stunned by the gruesome torture tools in the middle of the room than by the sign my eyes are drawn to. It hangs over a door with stairs leading out of the dungeon, proclaiming its ownership simply.

"MacKinnon Manor."

"No," I whisper in shock.

"No time!" Rhydian yells above the alarm.

"Aiden! Lucy! Aiden! Lucy!" Rhydian and Emily yell in chorus.

Lucy yells back and I can breathe again. We take the stairs out of the dungeon, following her voice to the floor above. This newer part of the building has tiled floors and proper walls. The recessed lights are lit by bulbs, not fire. The doors are square with peek-a-boo windows and openings at the bottoms for trays.

The alarm stops blaring. Rhydian runs down and knocks on all the doors, shouting my father's name.

"Lucy, move away from the door!" I use my magick to blast the door off its hinges.

Lucy uncovers her face. Tears are streaming down her cheeks.

"I can't walk," she says, pointing to her leg. It's splinted on each side. My magick lights up my skin and hums loud in ears. They hurt her!

"I've got her." Emily swoops in and picks Lucy up like she's a doll. Lucy pushes her face against Emily's shoulder and says "Thank you" over and over again.

Rhydian yells, "He's here, he's here!" He kicks down a door the old-fashioned way. There is movement sounding from outside the building and above us.

"I've got Lucy. I'm taking her back now," Emily says. She tries to transport, but nothing happens. "It must have a protection spell against transporting."

"Go back to the cell."

Emily takes off with Lucy, running in the direction we came from. Lucy's eyes are wide and she's shaking. "Don't stay, Willow! They want you!"

Emily is fast and even Lucy's weight doesn't slow her down.

I'm at the end of the hall where Rhydian has found my father. He's lying on a cot at the back of a small, square jail cell. He turns slowly so we can assess his injuries, and my magick flares at the sight of the bruises on his face. His right hand is discolored, swollen and puffy; surely the bones are broken. He coughs up blood before speaking.

"My smart girl." He reaches with his feeble good hand to touch my face.

"We've got to go," Rhydian says. "Is there another way out of here? We can't transport. Something is blocking us."

My father sits up slowly and cringes. "Maybe back through the older part. There should be a way outside to the grounds."

Rhydian is all business as he helps my father up and walks him out to the hall. The steps above us are louder now.

We start down the stairs when I hear Sabine's voice calling: "Wait, wait!"

I have no interest in speaking to her after what she's done. I thrust my hand upward to break the ceiling, and it crumbles down in grand fashion, complete with smoke and rock to block her path. A pipe bursts and water showers down. I don't bother to stick around, leaping down the stairs behind Rhydian and my father.

I use my hand to light the way in the old tunnel. There is no light beside my magick and I am beginning to wonder if we are heading in the right direction when the tunnel turns and starts to slope upward.

Outside light comes in through slats of wood in the door ahead. We start moving quicker and my father moans as he hangs on to Rhydian.

I throw a light ball at the door, busting it apart, and we run outside. We're at the edge of a forest. When I turn, I see the castle: MacKinnon Manor.

"Rhy! Wills!" Cross yells, running down the tunnel toward us in full armor with Quinn and Tullen. We're all outside now. It's damp and foggy.

"We transported as soon as Emily let us. She had to get Lucy home." Cross pats me on the back. "I'm so sorry, Wills. To think Sabine would do something like this to yer family—*her* family . . ." His face says it all.

My father struggles to breathe and Rhydian sets him down.

Father coughs. "I'm not sure it was her . . . not completely, anyway." He blinks several times. "It's all off. Something doesn't make sense. She was never present . . . the torturing . . . but the High Coven . . ."

I cringe at the word *torture*. Looking over my father, I can't help but think of what I saw in that dungeon. Lucy with a leg splint. My father spitting up blood, his body weak and broken. I gnash my teeth together and shake my head.

"Where's the guard of her estate?" Quinn asks.

In the same breath, we look up to see Sabine and a team of five walking across the acreage toward us. Her hair is flowing down her back, red like fire, and there's a look of concern in her eyes.

"It's a trick."

Rhydian puts a hand in front of me to keep me from walking to them. "She's part of the High Coven," he reasons. "Wait a minute and let's listen to what she says."

I can't believe his calm demeanor, but I take the advice. I take a deep, even breath, and it calms me—sort of. Someone needs to answer for taking my father and Lucy, not to mention the horrible condition in which we found them. My inner rage is building and I'm ready to go crazy, but, thanks to Mom, I decide to put it on tap until I need it.

CHAPTER 18

The grounds of the MacKinnon Manor are immaculate, several acres of lush green grass surrounded by forest. The manor itself is a modern-mansion-meets-castle. A black Lincoln Town Car comes down the drive.

We stand tense in the front yard—the royal Guardians, my father, and me. We're all waiting for Sabine's explanation of the fact that I just found my father and Lucy on her property, abused, tortured, and locked in an old dungeon. Sabine has several security guards with her, and neither of our groups seem like we want to talk.

"Who's coming down the drive?" Tullen asks. The way he's staring at the car, you'd think he could see right through it, but the blacked-out windows reveal nothing.

Sabine doesn't answer Tullen's question. "There must be a huge mistake," she says. "I didn't know. I truly did not know that part of the grounds was being used. My security is only set up in detail for the main house. That part of the property and the underground have been closed for years and only kept for their historical significance. The property is registered with the historical society. We only have alarms on the second floor in case of intruders or vandals." Sabine's face doesn't give much away.

I quirk my eyebrow at her.

Does she really think that I can believe this? That there could have been two prisoners held captive below her home without her knowledge? I look at my father to see him struggling. His stomach is bleeding and Quinn is bent over him, bandaging him up and using magick at the same time. I need to get him medical treatment. I could just transport us away and get him to safety.

Bam!

A light flashes at the back edge of the back of the property, radiating wide and strobing a couple of times. I blink to clear my eyes and focus, but I hear it first—a loud, slow clap coming from the woods.

"Excellent. Now the game is afoot. Here is my highly regarded evil Stepmother, trying to talk her way out of something devilish, I'm sure," Evan says, his voice mocking. "And my niece, naïve enough to believe that her grandmother would care about her." Evan approaches us, an army of demons and other magickal creatures close behind.

Sabine's hands cover her mouth. "But you're . . . you're—"

"Dead? I'm sure you'll continue to wish that was the case, especially with Willow here."

Evan is about twenty feet away. Cross, Rhydian, and Tullen make a barrier with their bodies between me and Evan. Quinn is checking my father's vitals and pulling things out of a bag next to him.

"Can you use magick to heal him?" Rhydian asks.

"No, I tried. They used curses!" Quinn replies. My father's face is tormented, his eyes dark.

"Evan, I don't understand. Did *you* do this?" I don't really want him to answer, afraid of the outcome.

"Being the bastard son of Harkin has some privileges—like blood." He spits the word as if it tastes rotten. "Sabine is the cause of many deaths. She's the orchestrator of many events, such as the accident that separated you from your mother." He points a finger between us. "The problem was, she was hoping to steal you away, but instead Nuala fought back and ended up dying. Good thing Daddy Dearest came along because he saved you from a similar fate."

Sabine's eyes are full of tears. "Don't talk about her! You have no right!" she yells.

Evan's voice echoes across the field. "Of course not. There are no rights for those who are not fully Wiccan. You'll always see to that, won't you, Stepmother?" He sweeps his arms out dramatically. "Welcome to the new world."

Evan waves his hand and the army waiting behind him yells, "Ooh-rah!"

The army is ominous—all broad muscles and

horns. Their skin is dark and varies in color, armor covering their thick bodies. The snarls on their faces and tensed shoulders show they're ready for a fight.

Evan smirks at Sabine. "I have every right because Harkin's contract was in place for me to be the next in line with a betrothal of marriage to one of the Noble Covens." He waves his hand in the air. "It didn't matter anymore that I was a bastard, a little different. But you saw it. You knew I wasn't full Wiccan!"

Sabine keeps looking from him to me.

"You had every intention of killing me, to be rid of the next in line. When that didn't work, you were responsible for the death sentence given to my Meghan." Evan's voice grows louder and his face tortured. "You had information that we married in secret. The question is, did you know about the baby!"

Sabine hangs her head. "I didn't affect his decisions like that. I tried at first, I admit, but all my children were gone. Liam left. Nuala and Aiden had taken Willow away from Edayri. You were our last child—" Her voice hitches.

"But not *your* child. Let's never forget that. You don't like anyone different. Meghan being anything but Wiccan made her less, made her life unworthy— kind of like me. You gave her a death sentence so you and Harkin could save the image of the crown and its royal traditions. That was a mistake. Holding power that shouldn't be restricted is not what the Horned God and Goddess would want, Sabine. Killing innocents? Tsk-tsk." He waves his finger back and forth.

Horned God? I haven't heard about him since I first looked at the Book of Shadows.

The demons rush the open lawn and yell, holding fists and swords aloft. There is a change in the air. I gravitate up from the grass and my magick comes to life, lightning and power licking all over my body. It feels like controlled static electricity, the tingling and hum becoming intense. I point to the front line of the army and they sail back in one motion, knocking over the next advancing group.

Sabine turns to me. "Willow, run! Take your father. This isn't your fight. I'm so sorry." Her hair picks up with the wind and she throws light balls at the advancing demons. Her security detail has some type of shockwave guns which they fire at the advancing army. I look back to witness my royal Guardians in full battle gear, swords drawn. They form a semicircle protecting my father.

A few of the demons are on the ground and Evan floats over them. He has powerful magick. I'm not surprised. He drops to the ground, and so do I. We're only about ten feet from each other. His eyes are changing color; horns peek through his hairline; his skin darkens; his canine teeth grow. "This reign needs to end, Willow. It's a secular monarchy that boasts nothing but destruction. You can't accept the crown —this family must destroy it! And if you stand in my way, well . . ."

Well, what? He will kill me? I can't believe that; he could have done that long before now. This is a vendetta against Sabine.

"Evan, look." I point to my father. "You are doing just what you want to rage against."

"No." He shakes his head. "Don't follow Sabine. That gives me only one choice."

"My mother will never forgive you." I hope it will give him pause.

Rhydian is beside me. "So, we're all just collateral damage, then? Destruction for destruction's sake? There has to be a better way."

Evan glances behind him. "Nuala is no longer here to judge me. I can't let this divisive reign continue."

Evan morphs into armor similar to that of the demons all around him, flexing it with his movements. His sword is thin like a samurai's. He advances toward Rhydian. I throw my hand out and hit Evan with a light ball, moving him back.

His menacing laugh echoes across the lawn. "Ah, are you protecting Rhydian now? You're saddling up to the vow and accepting it all?"

"Shut up, Evan, and let's fight!" Rhydian yells.

"All you Guardians are the same," Evan sneers. "You're all about the short game and forget the long game."

"No! You hurt my friend and my father! Is that your long game? This isn't a game!" I yell. "This is my fight!"

My anger swells my magick. My grief for Mrs. Scott; for leaving Daniel. My anger at this life and the manipulation of it all.

I'm done!

I conjure every bit of the emotion inside me—

disabling pain, hope, frustration, anger, love, sadness, regret—and I throw it straight at Evan in the form of a light ball. It hits and covers his body. Evan screams. His arms drop to his sides as he falls to the ground.

He will not be getting up.

The fighting around me continues. The demons are advancing to conceal Evan's downed body. Rhydian hits his wrist band and calls for reinforcements from the Guardians. They transport directly in front him and engage quickly with the demons and Sabine's security.

Lightning shoots across the sky, but not by my will. Emily, along with several warriors and another valkyrie, are suddenly in front of me, ready for battle. Emily winks at me before they charge the demons standing between me and the castle.

The roar of a large cat echoes from the edge of the forest. Marco must have brought support as well. A glowing light pulses as more demons enter in droves.

Quinn shouts at me, "Transport us to the hospital! He's dying. I can't help him. Someone has control near us and is making it worse."

"Put me down," my father coughs. I'm at his side on the ground and he touches my face. "Willow, my sweet girl. I release my magick—" I hug him in my arms and we're on the ground together. This can't be happening. This can't. He's broken, bleeding. His eyes plead with me.

"No! Don't do this. I can't lose you. I can get you . . ." Tears puddle in my eyes. I'm shaking. He's leaving me.

"Another did this . . . don't trust High Coven . . . Sabine . . . Evan . . . Evan is hurting. I'm sorry for . . ." His hand drops from my cheek. He takes a shallow breath and says, "I freely invoke my magick to my daughter, Willow Sola Warrington . . . in the Goddess's name. So mote it be."

And then his breathing stops.

"No!"

My screams echo and move everything around me in shockwaves.

I don't care.

I wail to the sky and curse it all.

I couldn't save Mrs. Scott; I couldn't save my father. The rain is tumultuous and mirrors my tears, my utter agony. I see nothing but us. My father in my lap, dead in my arms. My power is useless; I can't bring him back.

My family is gone. I'm alone.

A black magickal smoke surrounds us as it departs from my father and licks at me. I jerk away from the pain; it scorches my skin. His magick surrounds me and pulses at my skin. I scream in agony, my flesh burning, as I'm lifted into the storming sky. I don't want any of this, I want my father back!

The pain and hurt are never-ending. I embrace it. The smoke twists my body and turns me. I want to go with him—with my dad and my mom. My vision flashes a new scene, the car flips and flips; we land hard. I'm upside down. Someone pulls me out and throws me to the ground. She's out and reaching for me. A huge beast with wings is before me. A sword slices through the air; she grabs her neck. Red. Lots of red. A light. My father yells her name: "Nuala!" The beast yanks me to my feet. My father's face is stone-cold; his hands wave light from my mother to me. I fall and the beast explodes apart; I cover my small child face, before the vision changes where I am now. Throwing my arms wide, I open my mouth and swallow the black smoke to the sound of screams—echoes that are not my own.

The smoke clears and the rain stops. The fighting halts, all eyes on me.

Ants. That is what they are. To be stepped on.

The ground thunders when I drop to the ground. My vision is blurred, but I make out Quinn standing near my father. He is wide-eyed and holding his hands up. The darkness—it speaks to me, in my thoughts but not in recognizable voices, as if I'm split into two very strange and very powerful parts.

Make them pay. Make them feel the hurt, the pain.

Rhydian appears in front of me. "Willow?" He moves slowly, cautious, his hazel eyes worried, brows dipping with a question. I smell him, his scent like the ocean breeze. The beach . . . sand . . .

His lips are moving. He touches my arms and radiates warmth. My arms are no longer burnt but wisps of smoke hover around me. His pure magick, his voice, his comforting tenor speak only to me.

Willow, don't fight it. Accept it. Accept who you are becoming. Don't leave me, Willow. We are all broken. This is how the light shines through.

I breathe his name into my mind to shut out the other voice.

Rhydian.

I close my eyes and accept my father's immense, dark magick.

CHAPTER 19

The wind sings in my ears. I open my eyes to see an ethereal woman in a gossamer gown that clings to her perfect form. She is the Goddess. Waves of air and shifting spaces in my peripheral vision tell me that some of the fighters in the field are transporting away. Where Evan was is empty. Those who remain are on bent knee, including Sabine.

"I'm ready to take my place," I say.

The Goddess assesses me with her eyes. I'm sure I appear awful with dried tears and mud caked to my face, but I am more than my appearance. I am my mother, Mrs. Scott, and my father. There is no turning back.

She waves her hand and I'm wrapped in a light that is not my own. It turns and twists me in shades of white, pink, yellow, and blue. I gasp as I bend backward and forward. My hair flies in all directions. My arms lift from my sides and I'm covered in the sleek

Guardian armor, then morph back into my clothes, then into a purple cloak, and finally into my clothes again. I'm being weighed and measured for service by the Goddess. I feel judgment pass on the unwanted magick, but it is now accepted and owned. Dark and light have become one in me.

A female voice in my head speaks with authority.

You are the most powerful among them—the prophesied spirit element. Inexperienced in the realm of magick though you may be, they fear and respect you. Unite with all. The Convergence is coming.

Her face appears in the mist around me. She's beautiful. Her hair waves like the ocean, her face is like that of a Venetian angel sculpture, and her voice echoes so that all can hear.

"Willow Sola Warrington serves as Queen to the Edayri realm of magick royalty, in my name."

All below me answer in unison, "Blessed be."

I speak to the Goddess in my mind. *Thank you.*

Nothing lasts forever. Be of care, Willow.

I float down and land on the grass in bare feet. My clothing has changed to a gossamer gown and flowing purple cloak that dances behind and around me with the wind. My hair is waved. I've been presented in likeness to the Goddess, an honor not lost on me. I survey everyone around me on bended knee, heads bowed—Wiccan, demon, valkyrie, shapeshifter.

What do I say?

After a minute, Rhydian peeks up at me and winks. This moment is historical and epic, but I can't help it. In the gravity of the moment, I do exactly what I shouldn't: I giggle. A weight is lifted. Will I or won't I accept my predestined fate? It's all answered. It's done.

Those nearest look up at me and my cheeks heat. Eoin, the commander of the Guardians, shakes his head with a smile. I smirk at Rhydian. Time to honor the Goddess.

"You." I point to a demon who strikes me as someone in charge, a leader. I see it all over him—the confidence and bravado. He's taller than most, broad and muscled, dressed in armor that strains over his body to cover only his legs, arms, and back. His large horns sweep back and away with his long dark hair. He's adorned with markings on his chest and wears several long necklaces.

He comes forward, head held high and chest thrust forward. He represents a new magick I can invoke at my will. I sense his anxiety; it licks off him in waves that are almost delicious. I try to change my thoughts. The dark side is inviting and intrusive, so with a quick shake of my head, I steel my resolve.

"Do you challenge me without knowing me?" I ask.

He thinks about this, then replies, "Do you judge me and my kind without knowing us?"

The circle of waged hatred without knowledge or understanding hovers on the horizon, on the cusp of a tipping point.

"No, I don't. I'm an outsider to Edayri and the

prejudices of the past are lost on me, as they should be lost going forward. Don't you agree?"

The demon, his stature proud, smiles. Although it could appear evil, it's a genuine smile, and the emotions I feel running through him are clearly of acceptance. The magick is guiding me and I'm letting it.

"I do, Your Majesty."

He bows his head and the other demons follow his lead.

"The vendetta of vengeance is over. Take your wounded home. You and I shall meet again."

Rhydian tries to interrupt me, his brows creased. The demon in front of me pays him no attention.

"You're not afraid of—"

"Should I be?" I ask, flexing my hand and showing my magick. A guiding voice in my head says, Mark him.

He continues to smile, his fangs more evident as they peek through. "No, I don't think so."

"Your name?"

"Ax. Formally Thaxam."

"May I, Ax?"

He nods and I touch his hand. My mark appears, a royal brand in a scrolling design that burns his skin. He makes no noise of discomfort and doesn't let on if there's any pain, although I appreciate pain differently now and don't deny him the experience. The mark will allow me to call him to me, he will be part of the royal Guardians. It's not a two-way street, but this doesn't seem to bother him.

Rhydian's jaw is tight and his lips thin. He stares ahead over the other demons.

The demons follow Thaxam into the forest in silence and transport away. The Guardians are tending to the wounded and leaving as well. I scan for Emily and see her smiling, talking to warriors and Cross. I turn and see Tullen and Quinn smiling and talking.

This battle is over.

"Willow?" Sabine says my name tentatively.

I turn to her. She is grasping at her hands, her knuckles white, sweat on her brow. I should want to comfort her, go to her, but my disdain and hurt for what she's done to Evan, my mother, and me keep me where I am.

"I . . . I did not take your friend or your father and do this."

"I know." She was too busy fighting to continue to wield a curse that killed him.

Her shoulders relax. Sabine's security roughly brings forward the dark-haired High Coven member. "This is Celestia. She admitted to orchestrating the capture of your friend and father. She was working with Evan."

I don't think Evan would agree. Dad said he was hurting and he had plenty of opportunities to hurt or kill me, until today he took careful steps to show me magick. Celestia however, took whatever agenda she had beyond Evan.

Celestia pulls at the security guards holding her. "Get off me! I don't have to answer—"

Her voice! Now I can place where I've heard it before. My inhale is sharp.

"You, don't know the half of it! You're not fit to rule. Even the trigger from two years ago, didn't work." She pulls her arm from one of the security guards.

She orchestrated my assault at the age of fourteen. She was at my house. She's who Mrs. Scott was talking to—the woman in the cloak. She's the one who ordered her killed. The recognition is immediate.

Judge her.

"For me, Mrs. Scott, and my father," I say, devoid of emotion. Celestia's mouth falls open and she gasps as I let my magick warn her.

I lift my hand and quickly twist my fingers in command.

Her neck snaps. Celestia is no more.

The security guards drop her limp body. Her magick is released—all mine if I want it, but I don't. It is tainted with the memory of hurt and death. I direct it to the sky to empty it into the void.

Sabine looks like a deer in headlights. It is all I can do to swallow my tears back in anguish over the deeds of Celestia—the assault in the alley, the killing of Mrs. Scott and the torture that led to the death of my father. I feel justified in my actions . . . almost. I rub my hands on my clothes, wondering if it will clean me of my actions.

Rhydian's voice comes from behind me. "She killed Mrs. Scott, didn't she?" I nod. Sabine stands stunned and I turn from her to Rhydian. "She also tortured and cursed my father and caused his death."

Rhydian says something to Eoin, then comes to my side. I ask him to take me home. I'm drained of any more thoughts and actions. I don't care to behave in a way that is perceived acceptable. I hug him, my head on his shoulder, and I cry. I barely register him transporting us back to my home in Chepstow.

CHAPTER 20

I stand in the entrance of my house in Chepstow, Massachusetts, still hugging Rhydian. I lean my head away from his shoulder, but otherwise we don't move. I focus on the pentagram drawn on the foyer floor and the magickal staff leaning on the wall to the side. Although the blood from earlier was cleaned, the house is stained.

Welcome to your new life.

I'm numb at being the only one to come home. Mrs. Scott and my father will never walk down the stairs, never be in the kitchen or anywhere else in this house again.

"Can a blooded vow decipher my emotions?"

The look in Rhydian's eyes and a slight quirk of his lips tell me all I need to know.

He waves his hand and whispers words to put everything back as it should be. The round table is centered under the hanging chandelier with a vase full of flowers. The chalk is removed from the floor, replaced by an oriental rug under the table. The dirt and marks on the walls vanish.

Duke bounds in from the office, wagging his tail. I can't help but smile and waggle his ears. His dark fur is warm and soft as I hug him around his neck. He licks my face and I laugh through my almost dried tears. In the kitchen, I feed Duke and catch a glimpse of my reflection in the stainless steel refrigerator. My hair is brown. I pull it forward on my shoulder and examine the ends.

"It changed when you accepted his magick," Rhydian says. He's clean and back in street clothes now, jeans and a gray long-sleeve shirt.

"What else changed?" I ask, looking down at my body. I'm still wearing the white gown and purple cloak.

"Come."

Rhydian grins and takes my hand, leading me to the half bathroom down the hall. He places me in front of the mirror.

I look the same except for my hair, once dark blonde but now a chestnut brown resembling my father's. I touch it and think about him briefly. I lean forward and see that my eyes are still ocean blue like my mother's.

"Conjure your magick, Willow," Rhydian says.

I stare down at my fingertips and the design lights up and swirls around my fingers, hands, and arms. Rhydian gently tilts my chin up toward the mirror.

"Oh!" I gulp.

A design on my forehead pulses with the familiar

blue glow: an interwoven band that resembles a crown. I tentatively touch my forehead; the crown doesn't waver. I angle my palm and light shines into it. Rhydian is watching me in the mirror.

"Is this common?"

Rhydian grins. "No, but Willow Sola Warrington, nothing about you is common. You are very special. The Goddess crowned you directly today, and that hasn't been done since the beginning, to my knowledge."

As I let go of my magick, the hum and the blue designs fade from my body, including my crown. The moment feels intimate with Rhydian behind me in the closeness of the bathroom. I'm afraid to turn around with his assessing eyes watching me in the mirror.

A voice calls out: "Wills?"

Rhydian closes his eyes and backs out of the bathroom, making room for me to leave. It's Emily and Cross. They walk into the kitchen and Emily is hugging me before I even see her.

"Wills, I'm sorry about your father."

I hug her back. Cross speaks in a hushed voice with Rhydian.

"Willow, Sabine and the remaining members of the High Coven have been sequestered in Hallowed Hall and are under Guardian watch. Edayri is buzzing about the Goddess crowning you, your magick, and that you marked a demon general to your royal council. You have all the realm on your side. Everyone is waiting for you!" Her smile is infectious, reaching her eyes. She shakes my shoulders. "Wills, did you hear me?" She hugs me again. "I knew it!"

I pull back from her. "Lucy?"

Her voice drops in enthusiasm. "She'll be okay. She's home. I had her leg healed before I took her home."

"She isn't part of this world, is she?" I bite the inside of my cheek, waiting for Emily to respond.

Her bright eyes darken. "She doesn't know who she is, Willow. She's—"

Cross interrupts. "Another valkyrie?"

"And human. A dangerous combination. I've been with her for most of her life, protecting and watching her grow."

"You can't keep this from her," I say.

"I know," Emily answers. "But she could stay human too. I'm not sure if she will become more, but with your triggering, she could."

Rhydian's head moves to the side as if he's listening to something I can't hear. Cross does the same. I shrug my shoulders when Emily tilts her head at them.

"Cross?" Emily asks.

"Evan. The Guardians are reporting that he and others crossed into the rift here."

"Here? In Chepstow?" I wring my hands.

Rhydian shakes his head no.

"Where?"

"He's here on this plane, Willow. They say he was hurt in a bad way by whatever magick you pushed at him. They must be looking for a healer. Tullen thinks Cross and I might be able to track him."

"Don't." The mood of the room changes. "This is enough, Rhydian. If he comes for me, he comes."

Rhydian takes a step toward me. "That's not acceptable."

"He's my family, my uncle. Rhydian, he had plenty of chances to hurt me before now."

"You're not invincible, Willow. He could—"

I hold my hand up. "Stop. It's enough for now."

Rhydian tenses his jaw. The muscle ticks and he turns away from me. Cross doesn't reveal much, but his eyes glint toward me in approval before he speaks.

"Eoin, wants to meet with ya soon, but until then, he's ordered that we put protective magick around yer home and stay here on watch. Tullen and Quinn will relieve us and we'll take shifts."

Looking at Emily I ask, "Will you stay here too?"

"Duh. But to not protect you, you've got that shit in spades. I'm here to whip up my famous tacos and hang."

I laugh and hug her.

Five months later

Lucy pulls her car into my driveway. I run out into the snow flurries, bundled in my coat and school uniform.

"Hey. Looking a bit gloomy today," she says. "Need some pep up music?"

I shake my head. "Depends on the tunes. If I have to listen to Lukas Graham's '7 Years' one more time, I might blast this car apart."

She laughs. "Don't hurt my car. You know she doesn't control the tuneage."

We park in the school lot and Emily slides up next to us in her Camry. Getting out of Lucy's car, I pull my scarf around my neck a little tighter, breathing in the crisp, clean air. Spring will be here soon. Of course, that doesn't mean the snow stops in Chepstow.

"So, Lucy," Emily says, "did you tell her?"

"Tell me what?"

Lucy bites her bottom lip and keeps walking toward the school entrance. Emily smiles and fluffs her unruly short hair into a new mess. At our lockers, I stand next to Lucy tapping my foot, hands on hips.

"I got a scholarship."

"What?" I'm not surprised, but I pretend for Lucy. "What kind, exactly?"

Her grin stretches from ear to ear. "Stanford, full ride!"

I hug her and jump up and down with joy. Emily shakes her booty with us. Lucy is all smiles.

Coral and her cronies pass by as we celebrate. "Oh, look, the village idiots," she says.

Being snubbed by Coral just makes me more joyous, especially when she trips over her own feet. She recovers quickly.

Lucy pushes me. "Wills, don't."

Emily laughs. "Oh, come on. You can't prove it." Winking at me, she hooks her arm through mine and we walk down the familiar hall toward homeroom.

I told Lucy about my Wiccan heritage after the funerals for my father and Mrs. Scott. She took it in stride. I still haven't revealed the other part, though— the part about being crowned Queen. I made a pact with Rhydian and the Guardians to finish high school in as normal a way as possible. Having Eoin, the commander of the Guardians, move into my home isn't really normal, though. It does help to pass him off as my legal guardian, some long-lost uncle, so that

I can stay put in an effort to be normal until I have to go back to Edayri.

In homeroom, Daniel is seated at his desk. He grins at me and leans over to say something just as Mr. Brandt shuts the door and announces an assembly. We all shuffle down the hallways to the auditorium. Daniel sits next to me. Headmaster Chin starts with the spring semester schedule changes and announces the date and theme for prom, then dismisses us with good wishes for spring break.

Student enthusiasm for the next class is non-existent as they linger in the auditorium and hallways. I follow Lucy out of the auditorium. Daniel taps me on the shoulder to get my attention and I turn around just as Coral is walking by.

"So, I know we aren't together, but would you want to do the prom thing with me?" he asks.

Coral purses her lips together in a tight smile and stares me down as she passes.

"I'm guessing Coral was hoping for that invite," I say, pointing at her with my thumb. Daniel keeps his hopeful eyes on me.

His hand brushes his wavy hair back from his face. "Yeah, maybe. Just . . . most days I can't remember exactly why we broke up."

That hits me right in the heart. "Well, with going in different directions for college, I think it's best. You should ask Coral."

"Really?"

"What?" I hug my books to my chest.

"Who are you? You can't stand Coral, but you're

pushing me off on her?" Daniel rolls his eyes, confused, then smiles his easy way. "Will you be around at all for spring break?"

"No, I'll be with my grandmother in Europe," I say. "I leave in two days."

He nods as Marco strides over.

"Hey, Daniel! Stuart is getting a pickup game together. What do you say?"

They walk off together and I feel his disappointment. I'm upset with myself too. I'm pathetic; I should do something or act awful so that he hates me, so that I can keep him safe. I still care about him and trying to put distance between us when we're around each other is hard, especially when we share friends.

I head to Advanced English, which drags on forever. Like all the students, I'm waiting for the half-day bell that will free us for a week. Usually spring break is equated with warmth, but living up north, we're happy just for the sun to shine on our frozen faces. The news has been projecting snow for tonight.

I've been visiting with Sabine at the manor in the Ember region of Edayri and have learned that she experiences similar weather, as her location isn't that different from living in Ireland, where our Celtic heritage comes from.

My visits with Sabine have been good. We're trying to build a relationship. Our last conversation still rings in my mind: "The more entanglements you have there, the harder it will be for you here." I can't help but think of Daniel. I had planned to go to homecoming, prom—all of it. It's all wishful thinking now.

The half-day bell sounds after what feels like hours. I walk with Emily and Lucy to the parking lot.

"So, we're still on for girls' night?" Emily smiles.

I beam. "Yes! I've got a movie lineup and all kinds of junk food for us."

"As long as Ryan Reynolds is in one of those movies, I'm a happy girl," Emily says. "See you in a few!"

Lucy and I climb into her car and make the trip to my house. She parks in my driveway and says, "Will, would you be okay with . . . oh, never mind." She turns off the car. She looks nervous.

"What? Just ask."

"Daniel asked me to prom. I kinda said yes. Are you okay with that?" Her face is scrunched up. She's prepared for me to be angry. But I have no right to Daniel. All I can do is shake my head affirmatively. I hug her. She's my best friend and she deserves happiness, including someone as great as Daniel.

"It's fine, Lucy," I say, sounding more confident than I feel. I get out of the car, happy she'll be back later. It's just a dance. It doesn't mean they're together.

Duke greets me excitedly at the door. I waggle his ears, but then I smell something strange coming from the kitchen—smoke. I drop my backpack and run to the kitchen to find a fire.

"Eoin!" I yell. Duke barks in the background.

The fire grows from the stove. I wave the smoke

away and call my magick, thrusting my hands forward just as someone behind me pulls me backward. The fire extinguishes. A black bag comes down over my head and I'm dragged, screaming, back by my armpits. Bracelets are clamped to each of my wrists. My magick stops. I can't do anything, can't even find the ever-present hum.

I kick and yell, mentally reaching out for Rhydian, then Ax. Duke is barking. There's more than one person in the kitchen with us. I connect my foot with someone in front of me and they cuss. I'm being transported. I hear Rhydian's voice in an echo, calling my name. I'm pushed and pulled and twisted in the transport. My stomach drops as I hit the ground.

I try to push myself up, but the heel of a boot pushes me back onto hard dirt.

"Stay down," a young female voice says.

"She's not going to help us. She hates him," a male voice says. "They'll locate her."

"I've got this," another young woman says, and a sharp pain shoots through my head.

Lights out.

Get Your FREE Novella at
www.AuthorCMNewell.com
Rhydian, the youngest Captain of the Guardians,
learns the long-lost Wiccan Princess is about to be
the new Queen.

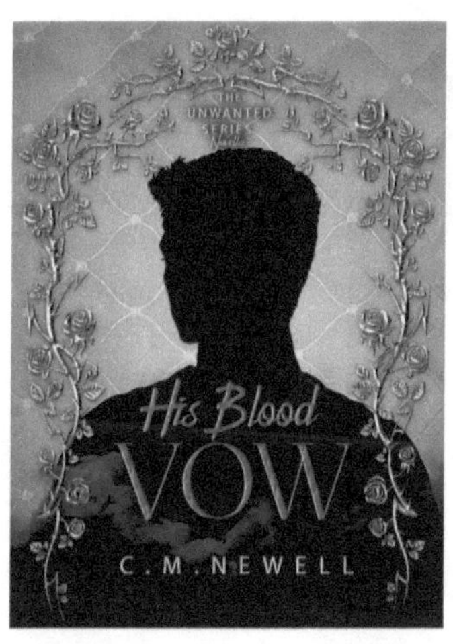

REIGN
Sneak Peek into Book II

My thoughts surface from the depths of a dark pool of nothingness. The first things I notice are the scent of rich earth and the feel of grass and dirt on the ground beneath me. These hold me steady. I smell smoke and hear the crackling of a campfire. I work to piece together my memory, a rush of blurry moments.

Barking. Duke is barking.

Smoke. A fire in the kitchen.

I'm yelling for Eoin, then being grabbed. My magick fails.

I'm being taken from my home. I fight, but there are more of them, and I'm in darkness; I can't see. I'm pushed, pulled—and then there's nothing left. My memories stop there.

I steady my breathing to avoid drawing attention. My first thought is of Rhydian, my royal Guardian, and blood-vowed protector. Should I reach out to him? That could make things worse, not knowing where I am. Rhydian would come armored with the rest of the royal armada, ready to kick butt. I shouldn't put any of them at risk until I know more. Heck, maybe I can escape on my own and get home.

Careful not to move my body, I squint my eyes to view my surroundings without alerting anyone that I'm awake. I don't hear anyone close to me. It's dark, but I can make out a campsite with a fire about ten meters away. The surrounding trees are tall and thick, more ominous than anything else, and possibly the best place to make a run for it. I make out some people—no, demons, with colorful skin and large horns that sweep back from their heads. There is no way for me to confirm where I am. It's possible that I'm still in Chepstow, Massachusetts, but I'm more likely in the magickal realm of Edayri. I open my eyes fully and confirm I am alone.

My body is stiff; my shoulder muscles scream because of the angle of my arms. Something weighs on my wrists behind my back. I'm still in my school uniform, the skirt twisted, but I can move my legs. I push against the heels of my purple chucks to sit up. The group near the campfire doesn't notice. A coldness comes over me. I've got to transport from here.

Holding my hands open behind my back, I mentally call my magick. I feel the familiar hum within me, but it won't rise beyond the surface. I twist to look over my shoulder and see the magick's familiar glow that should be flowing in patterns on my skin, instead contained in the glowing bracelets around my wrists.

I pull at the cuffs. My breathing is short and fast, and my eyes water as I attempt to shove the cuffs off. They don't move but instead pinch and twist on my skin. I yelp in pain. Someone at the fire turns my way.

I summon my magick again, then again.

Damn it, I need you!

I yank harder on the blasted bracelets and call to Rhydian in my mind. "Help me! Find me, please. They are coming!"

A jolt of pain travels up my arms in a snap. The connected cuffs release, and I can move my arms. The weight of each bracelet pulls my hands to my side as if each arm weighs ten pounds. My wrists glow like purple nightsticks. I could run, I think, or swing these heavy weighted bracelets at their heads. My magick shows itself on the surface of my skin more, but it's visibly muted and dull to my control; the patterns flow, ebb, pulse, and try to connect, but instead, the magick flows to these wicked bracelets!

Four young demons surround me; the opportunity to run into the trees is gone. These demons are dressed like anyone from my school, except they have colorful skin and small horns coming out of their heads. They keep a distance from me, observing the glowing bracelets.

A dark red female with short, black, spiky hair, wide dark eyes, and a taunting smirk gets closer to me. She's not so intimidating in her jeans, goth boots, and black anime hoodie.

"Your Royal Highness. You aren't much without it, are you?" She gestures to the glowing bracelets.

"Wanna test that?" I spit back, holding up the bracelets.

"Oh! So, you aren't helpless without your magick after all? How cute!" She claps her hands together, bats her eyes, and grins to reveal small fangs.

Cute? I'll show her cute when I use these heavy monstrosities on the side of her head!

The other three teenage demons move off to the side. A shorter male demon dressed in a dark tracksuit, which I hadn't noticed earlier, moves closer in my periphery. I turn on him, and he jumps back a step.

"What do you guys want with me?"

The girl demon seems to be the only one talking. "To correct what you fucked up!"

"What I—?"

A deep rumble of a voice interrupts and captures our attention. A dark figure emerges from what appears to be a tent on the other side of the campfire. The horns are more substantial, not some teenagers. My heart pounds faster, and the chill of the air makes me shiver. The figure becomes familiar as it gets closer.

Theon.

Theon is tall and lean, a cross between a grunge twenty-something and a samurai. He's a skilled fighter and usually near my uncle. Like my uncle, he is half Wiccan and half-demon.

His long hair is messy and obscures most of his face, but I can tell that his jaw drops at the sight of me. Marching in big strides, he focuses his attention on the feisty demon in front of me. "What the hell have you done, Sikkori?"

"We did what needs to be done. She's right here." Sikkori gestures to me with painted neon pink claws.

"No, you've complicated it more! The Guardians and the whole royal wiccan armada will be looking for her! Do you ever use your brain?" Theon pushes his hand through his hair and over his horns in visible frustration. He grabs Sikkori's arm and pulls her away. He points at the shorter demon to the side of me, who nods in some unspoken agreement.

"Please come with me and get warm by the fire,"

the shorter demon says in a small voice matched by a half-hearted smile. I follow him, watching Theon hover over Sikkori's tensed body.

I'm guided to sit on a large, fallen tree trunk. The childlike demon seems satisfied and gently touches my shoulder, almost bowing his head before he leaves.

He knows who I am and at least doesn't harbor the same irritation Sikkori seems to.

Theon raises his voice. "This camp location is in jeopardy now. It's not simple to just drop her off!"

Sikkori looks like a teen girl being scolded by a teacher. She rolls her eyes before pushing back. "So, she stays then!"

"And this is why. You asked. This is why you don't have more responsibility!"

Looking around, I see more tents scattered through the trees. I don't have a clear path to run. I give up on calling my magick; I can't use it because of the bracelets, and I can't seem to connect to Rhydian. I'm stuck.

I'm staring ahead, trying to formulate a plan when someone sits next to me. He's quiet and goes unnoticed by the few nearby because everyone is watching Theon and Sikkori. I know exactly who he is before I turn my head. This was the intel the Guardians had; this was why Sikkori brought me here.

Evan, my uncle, was presumably complete with the mental madness I caused by hitting him with magick during the battle at MacKinnon Manor.

He stares straight ahead like I'm not right next to him. I can't move. My uncle is . . . different. He's unkempt and messy, his eyes unfocused, nothing at all like himself.

I tentatively whisper his name. "Evan?"

The corner of his lip pulls up in recognition of his name. Without looking at me, he nods toward the arguing Theon and Sikkori. He waits until Theon throws his hands up in frustration, then speaks.

"Why is my niece here?"

Silence.

Theon walks in smooth strides to stand in front of Evan.

"Why is she here? No one said anything about this being the next step in our freedom, although plans do change."

Freedom?

"They just wanted to help you. The magick—" Evan holds his finger up, and Theon stutters before continuing: "Um . . . gift. The gift Willow gave you. They just want you . . . whole."

Sikkori hugs her body, looking younger. How old is she? I realize she must be younger than me at seventeen, although I feel like I've aged five years in several months since starting my senior year.

Evan doesn't respond. I break the uncomfortable silence. "Gift? What gift?"

"At the battle on the MacKinnon grounds, you sent uncontrolled magick that hit Evan. It was charged by your emotions, and it injured—ah, changed Evan."

Evan stands and sweeps his arms in a wide circle, spinning like a little child. "Freedom."

Everyone stares at Evan in the silence.

"The gift of seeing—understanding. The gift of redemption within myself and of knowledge. I hate, I love, I have anger and compassion, all rolled into one." Evan drops to one knee in front of me, and I scoot back, scraping the backs of my legs. I look everywhere but directly at his waiting face until he touches my knee. "It's freedom. I do not control it. It is only glimpses of the future. A wonderful gift from my niece."

I don't like this. How can I undo something I didn't know I was doing in the first place? What will they do to me if I make it worse?

"Ah, to be so young. Don't be burdened by the battle of doubt in your head," Evan says with a laugh. "No worries, Willow. I will keep my gift of sight, regardless of what the younger Emissaries' good intentions are."

"Emissaries?"

"Yes. That's us." Evan gestures in a big sweeping motion with his arms. Theon is assessing me with his scrupulous eyes.

I'm not sure what I should be more frightened of —the abduction to help Evan or the fact he doesn't want it. Either way, I'm limited with these bracelets.

Evan snaps his fingers, and the spellbinding bracelets break.

Did he just read my mind?

Evan offers his hand; I take it and stand. Theon rushes toward us, yelling for us to stop, and in a blur, he is gone. Evan is magickly transporting us. I gently pull my hand away, but I can't budge his steady grip. My feet land on solid ground and my stomach immediately turns with the abrupt guidance of the transport.

"Don't leave quite yet," Evan says, almost asking and hopeful.

Cold air sweeps around and chills me; the temperature is freezing. Cars sound in the distance. Though it is still dark, I can make out a colorful jungle gym among the dry winter grass. There are gravel walkways lined by leafless trees. Before I open my mouth, Evan waves his fingers and chants, covering me in warmth with new clothes—a thick puffed jacket, wool hat, and gloves. He has dressed for the cooler climate in a long, formal, black wool jacket and leather gloves. His horns, still visible, blend into his wavy hair.

"Why should I stay? Last time I saw you, Evan, I was collateral damage. Remember?"

"I wouldn't have."

I believe him, but it doesn't change the fact that the Guardians and Sabine don't believe that.

"Where are we, Evan? When can I leave?"

He squints and looks all around us, then stops and points over my shoulder. "Ah, there it is. Look."

The tip of the Eiffel Tower is a distant silhouette against the evening sky. So that's where we are. I have a sense of déjà vu that I can't connect.

"You were not born yet, when your parents took a stand against dear old dad. Later, I believe your father brought you here a few times." His smile turns from joy to sadness. "I needed to bring you away from the

Emissaries. I must protect them; the Horned God would want that. You also need to see and understand this place because of its ties to my sister. The history is important for you and your future, and for the Emissaries."

I have so many questions. I settle on the most immediate one. "Who are the Emissaries?"

"They are equality seekers."

"Who is the Horned God?"

"Quite simply, me." Evan laughs, and his horns glow just a little.

Okay . . .

"So, my Wiccan Queen and niece, what shall we do? Oh, yes—first, the warnings. Never run with scissors or knives unless your intention is to harm yourself and those around you."

He wobbles on his feet, and I back away with one big step. This is becoming even more strange than it already was.

"Evan? Are you okay? You seem . . ."

I can't bring myself to say it. Even's eyes, his face, look happy and carefree. He's different, but I'm different too. So much has happened since we first met under his guise of a therapist. He helped me connect to my magick and learn about my heritage. I look at him, and I long for my mother, my father, and the life that was normal—or more normal than this, anyway.

"So, do you recognize this place? Is it a place that calls to you, like a raven in another life?" He takes a deep breath and closes his eyes as if savoring the memory of something.

"Evan, why did you bring me here? It may be familiar, but I don't understand."

What's his intention? Is he going to let me go?

"We are tied together. Not physically, but the Goddess and the Horned God—we are their embodiment."

"How is that?" I breathe into my gloved hands and watch the chilled air turn white.

He laughs. "We are evolving and new." Evan waves his gloved fingers as if they are wings and his body moves by flutters in and out of my vision. "The caterpillar experiences the most evolution but its end result, the butterfly, has a lifespan that isn't very long."

What do I say? This is so weird.

"Remember this place, Willow. Ask Sabine about it. Consider what noble covens want and why. Don't be the status quo. Be a different Queen."

My mouth is dry. I don't know what to say to him. I want to be the right kind of Queen, but I can't be something I'm not. It strikes me that those teenage demons were worried about Evan. He's important enough they came for me and risked their lives. I could easily take the Guardians to them and have them all arrested or worse, but I won't do that. I can't do that.

"Call to Rhydian through your blood vow."

I need more from him besides my freedom. "Wait. Tell me more about this place before I leave. Why bring me here? How is it connected to my mother?"

He closes his eyes briefly. "This is where your father and mother took a stand against the Wiccan crown and the rule of betrothal. The place where we all flee toward a beacon of light." Evan points to the Eiffel tower in the distance and pulls his scarf closer to his neck. "The High Coven is not one to trust, but —" He laughs before continuing, his canines showing. "You already recognize that. Good girl. Don't let Sabine's perfect exterior fool you into thinking it mirrors an authentic interior. Chaos follows her—a type that is not only harmful but deadly."

I see it as soon as he says the word "deadly" his grief in a conjured vision of my mother and another lady I imagine was Meghan, his wife. She was killed by order of my grandfather, the Wiccan King, Evan's father. If it wasn't so cold and the light was better, I believe I would see tears gathering in his eyes.

"I'm sorry, Evan." I mourn as he does, for my mother, Mrs. Scott, and my father.

"You cannot have a funeral for someone without having a funeral for yourself." He shrugs, then says, "I'm sorry for all the losses we experience. Life is death, and death is life."

His eyes are haunted as they look everywhere but at me. Evan's weird riddles and words are true. I buried part of myself in the loss of my father, his death coming just as we were connecting, and he was sharing magick with me.

"Back into the mouth of the monster you go. Slay the dragon. If not, our time together may be brief."

His riddles sound like a threat and a warning at

the same time. The sincerity of his worry is something I don't doubt.

Who is the dragon I must slay?

Evan transports himself, his presence is gone too soon. Despite wanting to get home, I turn toward the jungle gym. He said so much that I don't completely understand, but the fact that this place is significant because of my parents gives me a reason to look around. I walk to a stone bench on the small greenway facing the jungle gym, pulling the collar of the coat closer to my neck. The cold wind whips my long hair and surrounds me in the quiet of the night.

A bronzed memorial plaque on the bench catches my eye. Summoning my magick to my fingers, I use the light to better see the inscription.

In memory of Nuala Warrington.

I remember so little of her. I take off my gloves and touch my mother's name as if that will bring me closer. I sit on the stone bench and tuck my hands into the warm pockets of the coat. I could easily transport myself home, but instead, I silent my mind and call to Rhydian as Evan directed me. I reach through space for the bond that connects us and comprehend his immediate connection and anguish.

The breeze on my face is instant. New warmth radiates from three royal Guardians who surround me in full armor and defensive stances.

Rhydian turns and I stumble to speak. "No one is here . . . um . . . besides me."

Cross's face drops from a scowl to a frown.

Tullen speaks first. "Willow, where have you been? It's been almost two days."

"I was taken by Emissaries and released by Evan, who took me here," I say with a shaky voice pointing to the plaque. Tullen reads it and touches my shoulder gently.

Rhydian hasn't moved. He's watching me as if he can't believe I'm in front of him. Finally, he speaks. "Cross, Tullen, search the park to see if there are any signs of magickal transport signatures."

"We arrived over there." I point to the spot where Evan brought us. "I don't think you'll be able to track him. Can we talk at my house? I just—want to go."

There is no verbal agreement, only Rhydian's outreached arms. The enveloping hug comforts me and releases the pit in my stomach. My tears fall without notice, and all I can do is breathe steadily in relief as Rhydian transports us to my front door in Chepstow, Massachusetts.

I don't release him, burying my wet face in his armored chest. Rhydian lifts my face gently to his and lays the sweetest kiss on my forehead. The moment is too brief. His forehead rests on mine in a physical and emotional connection that doesn't feel like a forced blood vow.

"I was so worried, Will. I couldn't sense you, and it was Evan all along. This could've been so much worse." Rhydian's statement is heavy on the cold night air.

"It was other Emissaries who grabbed me. Evan is

—different." How do I describe him without sounding crazy myself? I'm not even sure who to trust from his warnings.

"Why would you trust Evan? I don't care how different he seems; you agree he's partly responsible for Mrs. Scott and your father. Why are you wavering?"

The deaths of Mrs. Scott and my father are what Rhydian really wants to say—that Evan had a direct hand in what happened to my family. The twisted part is that Evan is my family. He's my uncle. Evan didn't kill anyone, Celestia did. She was responsible for Mrs. Scott's death and the torture and, ultimately, the death of my father. But I'm the killer that enacting justice on her. Deep down, when someone points out Evan's dark nature, I see that it mirrors my own—the dark voice I hear luring me from time to time.

"I don't believe Evan is a threat."

But do I really believe that?

ALSO BY C. M. NEWELL

The Unwanted Series

Magick

His Blood Vow (Exclusive)

Reign

Sacred

For more details please go to the website:
www.AuthorCMNewell.com

ABOUT THE AUTHOR

C. M. Newell is an award-winning YA fantasy author, receiving the 2016 New Apple Fantasy Award for her debut novel Magick in The Unwanted Series.

C. M. is a lover of all things fantasy and fairytale, especially the twisted ones. She loves to write strong female characters who don't fall victim to circumstance but instead rise above. C. M. prefers a world where a princess can save herself.

Originally from Tennessee and a nomad from various states and countries, she now calls home to sunny Florida with her family.

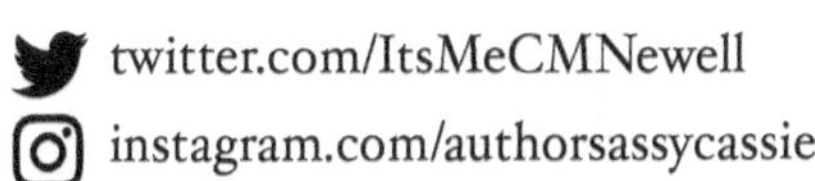

twitter.com/ItsMeCMNewell

instagram.com/authorsassycassie